The Running Game

The Running Game

Reachers Series Book 1

L. E. Fitzpatrick

Copyright (C) 2016 L. E. Fitzpatrick
Layout design and Copyright (C) 2019 by Next Chapter
Published 2019 by Beyond Time – A Next Chapter Imprint
Cover art by http://www.thecovercollection.com/
This book is a work of fiction. Names, characters, places, and incidents are the product of the author's imagination or are used fictitiously. Any resemblance to actual events, locales, or persons, living or dead, is purely coincidental.
All rights reserved. No part of this book may be reproduced or transmitted in any form or by any means, electronic or mechanical, including photocopying, recording, or by any information storage and retrieval system, without the author's permission.

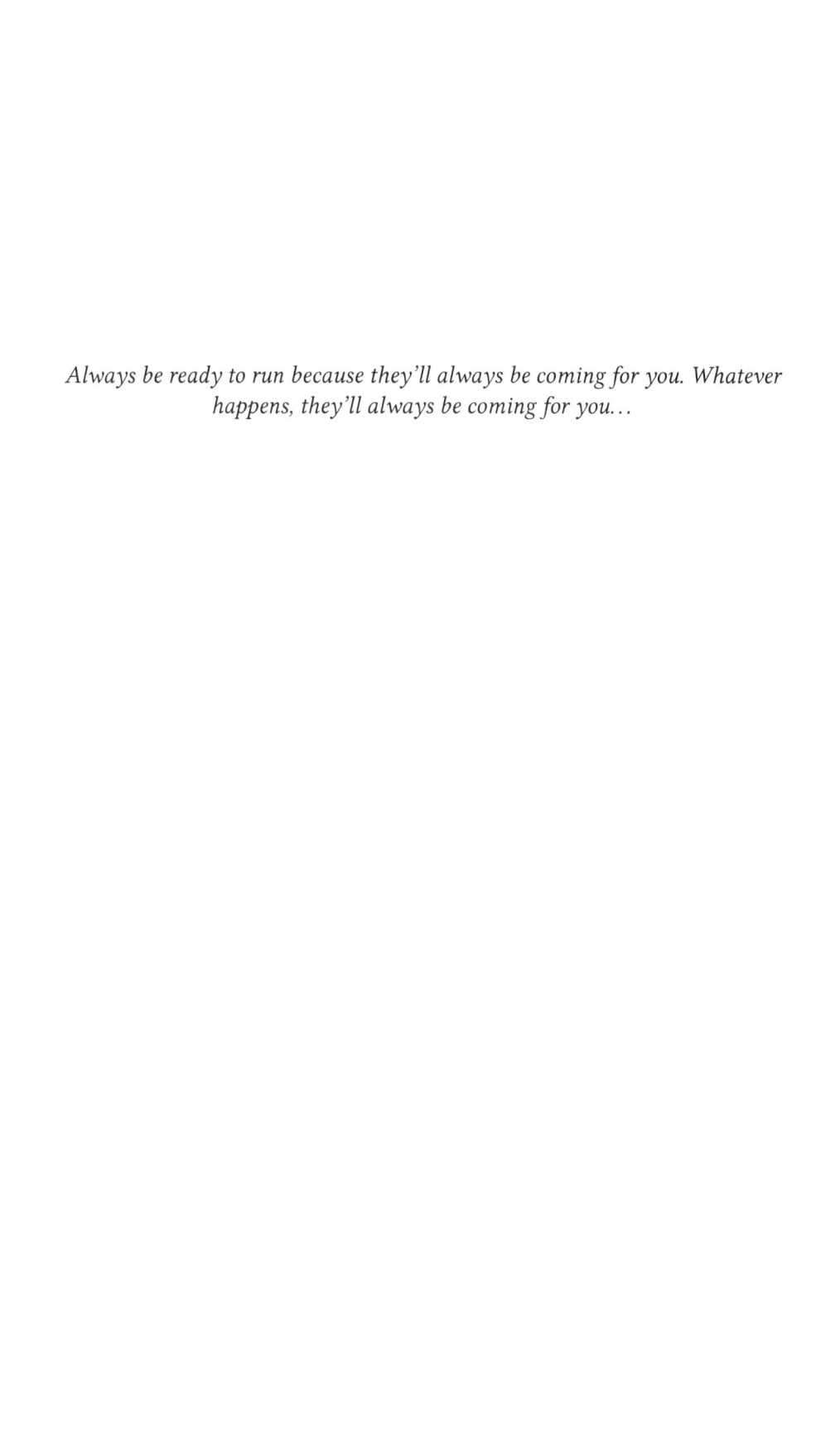

Always be ready to run because they'll always be coming for you. Whatever happens, they'll always be coming for you…

1

Five past eleven.

Rachel's shift should have finished three hours ago. She slammed her time card into the machine. Nothing. She gave it a kick, then another until it released, punching her card and signing her out for the night. The hospital locker room was unusually quiet. There was a nurse signing out for the night, two doctors signing in. Nobody spoke to each other–it wasn't that kind of place. Grabbing her threadbare coat from her locker, she drew it over her scrubs–the only barrier between her and the unforgiving October night. She walked through the ER waiting room, eyes fixed on the exit. You had to ignore the desperation. Three hours over a twelve hour shift, you had no choice but to pretend like you didn't care. Push past the mothers offering up their sick children like you could just lay your hands on them and everything would be better. Push past the factory workers bleeding out on the floor. Push that door open and get out. Get home. You had to. In six hours the whole thing would start again.

The first blast of cold air slapped the life into her aching body. The second blast nearly pushed her back inside. She tightened the coat around herself, but the icy wind still managed to weave its fingers through the thin material and loose seams. November was coming, and coming fast. She quickened her pace, trying to outrun the winter.

She hurried past the skeletal remains of another fallen bank, a relic of the days before the economy crashed and the country went to hell. Now the abandoned building housed those left to the streets: the too old, the too young, the weak, the stupid. Cops would be coming soon, moving them on, pushing them from one shadow to another until dawn or death, whichever came first. But for now they sat huddled around burning canisters, silently soaking in the heat as though they could carry that one flame through winter. They didn't notice Rachel. Even the most evil of men lurking in the doorways, waiting for helpless things to scurry past, overlooked the young doctor as she made her way home. Nobody ever saw her. At least they never used to.

Three – two – one.

Nine past eleven. Right on cue.

She felt someone watching her. It was always the same place, opposite the third window of the old bank. He was hidden, not in the bank but close. So close she could almost feel his breath on the back of her neck. She'd watched muggings before, these were desperate times and people took what they could when they could. There were rapes too, five this week, at least five that had needed medical care. It was a dangerous city and getting worse. But this was different. He–and for some reason she knew it was a he–did nothing. For a week he had been there, never betraying his exact position or his intentions, but she could feel him and the longer he waited the more he tormented her. He knew where she lived, where she worked, the route she took to the exchange store. And he escorted her home each night without ever showing himself. It made no sense. And that made it so much worse.

She wasn't intimidated easily; doctors in St Mary's couldn't be. It didn't matter that she was only five feet tall and looked like a strong wind would knock her down; she could still take care of herself. But the stalking had spooked her. The sleepless nights followed as she wondered who he was, what he wanted, if he knew.

There was nowhere for her to go in the city, no place she could hide, no escape. If she wanted to eat she had to work, and he would be waiting for her outside the hospital–watching, doing nothing. She was tired of it, tired of everything, but there was something she could do. She could make it stop, one way or another. Whatever he had planned, whatever he wanted to do to her, he would have to look her in the eye as he did it, because she was done running.

She stopped walking and turned.

The street was empty. But she could still feel him there. The buildings pressed their darkness into the street and the spattering of hissing lamplights did little to expose the nocturnal danger below. There was noise. There was always noise; voices, vehicles, the persistent buzzing of the electricity struggling to reach the edges of the city. So much going on, yet so little to see–a perfect place to hide.

"Okay you pervert," she whispered to herself. "Where're you hiding?"

The road stretched back into a tightrope. Gingerly, her feet edged back towards the ruined bank. She scanned the buildings around her, the upper windows, the ground level doorways, waiting for him to pounce. One step, two steps. Look. Nothing. She retraced her steps to the next building. Then the next. He felt so close–why couldn't she see him?

"You want me, well here I am, you freak. Come and get me!"

There was a shout from the bank. Someone running. A man. Her stomach clenched. She braced herself. He pushed by her, hurrying away. It wasn't *him*.

She turned, her eyes trying to make sense of what she was seeing. Then warm breath touched the back of her neck.

"Get down!"

The world went white.

With her face pressed into the filthy, cold road, Rachel waited. The ground beneath her trembled, but that was it. She frowned, waiting for something, trying to understand what she was doing lying in a stinking puddle at the side of the road. Hands were lifting her to her feet. She turned to the bank, but it was gone. Flames licked at the pile of rubble in its place. People stumbled from the wrecked building, choking and coughing, others with their eyes as wide as their mouths. But there was no sound, just staggered movement and growing heat. Rachel watched, feeling more curious than afraid. The silent panic was fascinating. She made to move and her ears exploded with noise. The shock of it knocked her back. Screaming, cries for help, the ringing of sirens came from every direction.

The ground shook again and the building exploded another mortar firework into the street. She felt her body being tugged away. But people were coming to help. People were still alive. She was a doctor, she was needed.

"I can help these people," she shouted trying to fight off the man holding her back.

"It's a lure bomb." The voice was so cool it made her freeze. She looked at the stranger and swallowed the clumps of gravel lodged in the back of her throat. She had wanted to meet him face to face but not like this.

He stared at her with blank eyes. The dead and dying meant nothing to him. He was there for her and her alone. His hand still held her shoulder, holding her back. The hand that had pulled her to safety. So many questions ran through her head but she could only push one out.

"A lure bomb?"

A small explosion that drew in the police, she raced to remember. *Followed by the bigger bomb that would blow them to pieces.* She turned back to the space where the bank should have been. More people were rushing to help, pulling at the arms and legs of the buried. If they were lucky bodies would come with them.

"We have to warn…" The man had gone.

The sirens grew louder.

Rachel drew in a steadying breath. *Three hours over a twelve hour shift – you have no choice but to pretend like you don't care.*

She started to run.

2

Charlie jolted awake in his chair, his face sodden with sweat. He wiped his forehead with his sleeve. Pain coursed up his back, reminding him of his nightmare. The recurring dream of the day it all went wrong. He fumbled through his pockets until he found his pills. The placebo was instantaneous, and the pain relief followed shortly after. He rubbed his eyes and returned to the camera positioned towards the apartment in the opposite tower block.

The lights were on, curtains open. Someone had come home and he'd missed it. His one job and he'd screwed it up. He kicked out at the crutch resting against his chair and watched as it skidded across the floor out of his reach. Flexing his hands he willed the crutch back to him. Nothing happened.

"Shit."

He lifted himself from his chair too quickly and his right leg buckled, knocking over the camera – only the most expensive bit of kit they owned. The lens cracked.

"Shit, shit, shit." He shouted from the floor. The shockwaves of pain started to subside. Anger and shame fought their usual battle, while the voice inside his head urged him to just quit already. And, as usual, a persistent nagging from his bladder brought everything into perspective. He carried a lot of indignity on his shoulders, the last thing he needed was to be found sitting in a pool of his own piss.

This wasn't how his life was supposed to be. Charlie Smith had been a legend. He was a Reacher, born with incredible powers and an arrogance that made anything possible. With his former self firmly in his mind, he rested his head on the floor and focused on the crutch again. His fingers stretched out, reaching for the plastic handle in his head. He could still sense the weight and feel of it with his powers, but to move it took an effort his brain struggled with. This should have been easy, but his telekinetic powers were failing him. The camera shook, turned on its side and then stopped altogether. The effort was exhausting and embarrassing.

Slowly, because nowadays everything had to be done slowly, he edged himself over to his crutch and, with it in hand, he managed to make it to the bathroom. It was a small victory, but it was nearly enough to cheer him up. That was until he caught sight of himself in the broken mirror fixed above the sink. He used to have charisma. He used to be able to smile his way out of trouble. Now he was lucky if people didn't cross the street to avoid him. Greying hair, dull red eyes, pallid skin. He was thirty-three; he looked fifty; he felt like a pensioner. The great Reacher Charlie Smith–reduced to this. Things had changed so radically in just a year. One year, two months, and eight days.

The lock in the front door turned. Charlie straightened his clothes. Everything was normal, everything was fine. He could cope, of course he could cope. He checked his smile in the mirror and stepped out of the bathroom as his brother kicked open the door and then kicked it closed again, to make his point.

"Everything okay?" Charlie asked.

His younger brother wore a scowl so deep it could have been chiselled into his skull. Everything was clearly not okay. But with John it was impossible to tell how far up the disaster scale the situation was. Charlie had seen that same scowl when a job went sour and he'd seen it when someone spilt coffee on John's suit.

"What happened?"

John glanced away. He was annoyed with himself – never a good sign. Charlie braved a crutch-supported step towards him. There was a four year age gap between the two of them. and it had never been more apparent.

Charlie gestured for them to sit down at the fold-up table in the dining space. Most of the time John had everything under control. It was rare for him to make mistakes or miscalculations. and when he did he would beat himself up over it for days. He would need Charlie, a professional in screwing things up, to put everything into perspective.

"She saw me," John confessed.

"She saw you!" Charlie said in disbelief. "You're like a creature of the night, how the hell could see you? Jesus, most of the time I don't even see you and I know you're coming."

John's fists clenched and unclenched. He stood up to work off the tension and started to pace; short, quick steps, squeaking his leather shoes against the linoleum floor.

"There was an explosion. Some bastard left a lure bomb right on her route. I had to pull her away before the goddamn building fell on her."

Charlie pinched the bridge of his nose. Even when his brother messed up he still managed to do something right. "What you mean is you saved her?"

John glared at him. "You're missing the point."

Charlie rolled his eyes. Only John would get himself so worked up over saving the life of their mark. "Listen, do you think he'd pay us if he found out we let her die?" Charlie said.

"You don't know that. We have no idea what he wants her for!"

It was true, they didn't and the fact was starting to chafe. The infamous Smith Brothers always knew the cards on the table before the deck was even dealt. Charlie planned jobs like he was writing a script. Nobody ever missed a cue. At least that was how it used to be a year ago. A year, two months, and eight days. Since then the jobs had dried up. They were lucky to get the Rachel Aaron case and that was only because Charlie's old mentor put in a good word for them. But luck and even the backing of an old priest didn't make the unknown any less troubling. They were out of their depth and they were still only in the shallows.

"Maybe he wants her dead," John stated.

"If he wanted her dead he would have asked us to kill her," Charlie replied. "And if he wanted her dead he wouldn't be approaching a priest to see if he knew anyone who could find her. He wants her found John, that's all."

"I don't like it," John snapped. "This whole job feels off."

"I know." Charlie took a deep breath, his next sentence shouldn't have made him nervous but it did. "Which is why I'm going to do a little field work myself."

John never looked surprised, or happy, or anything other than mildly impatient, but when something pleased him his right eyebrow would lift ever so slightly. As it rose, Charlie felt a pang of guilt that he hadn't said it sooner.

"I thought you were a liability," John jibed.

"It's surveillance in a hospital John, who's going to blend in better, me or you?"

The eyebrow perched higher on John's forehead. He'd been patient with Charlie, more patient than Charlie felt he'd deserved, waiting for his brother to get back in the game instead of going out on his own. John hadn't lost his edge. He didn't have a problem with stairs. He could drink what he wanted. Sleep when he needed. There was nothing wrong with his abilities. Charlie was holding them both back, but he knew John still clung to the hope that one day Charlie would recover and things would go back to normal. And Charlie needed him too much to tell him that was never going to happen.

"You sure about this?" John asked.

"We need the money."

"What if he does want to kill her, or worse?"

Despite what Charlie had said it was always a possibility. They weren't working for the good guys on this one and the girl had been hard to find, even with Charlie's powers. It was not going to end well for her and maybe that was why Charlie hadn't asked enough questions.

"We need the money," Charlie assured him. "That has to be our priority." That wasn't him talking. Sure he'd done questionable things, bad things even, but he had morality and right now it was screaming inside his head that this was all wrong.

John nodded, and Charlie was relieved to see that John was sharing his sentiments. "Fine, but if it has to be done I'll do it."

"No, you don't need this on your conscience. I'll do it."

John gave him a look. "Are we seriously going to argue about who gets to kill her?"

"Has to," Charlie corrected. "When you say 'gets to kill her' you kind of make it sound like a bonus prize. And no, we're not going to argue because I'll do it." He didn't have to say because it was his fault all of this had happened – that was a given.

John folded his arms. "Okay, but I get to dispose of the body."

Charlie scowled. "Did you mean to say 'get to'?"

His brother smirked. He had a unique sense of humour.

3

It took eight years for the British Empire to fall.

Like dominoes, major players in Europe and the western world started to topple, one by one. Each country falling hard enough to ensure the chain reaction was cataclysmic across the globe. Historians disagree where the trouble started; some argue it went as far back as the second world war when the powers in charge set to picking up the broken pieces of the world and gluing them back together. Others are more cynical, claiming that man was destined towards devastation as soon as the first communities were formed by primitive apes.

However it happened, the cracks had been under the surface for a long, long time, growing weaker and more unstable. Internal conflict kept many countries in a stalemate. Where poverty and war still had a stronghold the effect of what was about to happen would barely touch the Richter scale. But in places like America, France, and Britain, places that had settled comfortably into peace and grown rich from their warring neighbours, the disturbance would be off the charts.

It was the financial crisis that struck the first blow. Each country struggled to balance its homeland cashbook, taking more credit and lending out money until the value of currency plummeted. When the system fell apart civilised government started to crumble, unable to compromise political greed and public integrity. The people revolted, seeing big cats in the big cities squandering money while their families starved in the suburbs. In France and Britain the rioting lasted five years, erupting into a burst of devastating civil war. Places like Red Forest and further north became impassable trenches of conflict that even the militia couldn't conquer.

The civil unrest was brought to a temporary halt when disease started to spread through Yorkshire and Lancashire. Birth deformities, viruses, and contamination concerns separated Britain into two halves and all who could fled south to escape the troubles. Northern Britain was abandoned and even Wales and Cornwall found themselves lost in isolated beacons out of London's reach. Disease spread, terrorism battled prejudice, and before anyone had realised it, aid packets were being flown over from Germany and the Australians were holding rock concerts for British kids in poverty. Most of the country slummed, counties broke off, and suddenly all that anyone seemed to care about was the thriving capital, where business men still wore Armani and sipped espressos. And that was the hardest pill to swallow; despite what was happening less than a hundred miles away, London was still thriving in a modern utopia.

People fled to the great city; their safe haven which grew like a tourniquet around London. Looking to fill the rumoured jobs and sample the last remnants of the good life, most found, when they got there, that London was walled off with wire fences as tall as the buildings they were enclosing. The cops kept watch and if you couldn't pay, you weren't coming in. The gathering crowd clustered and culminated, and eventually Safe Haven, or S'aven as the locals called it, became a city in its own right; a city with rulers as powerful as any of the fat men sitting in parliament square, and just as ruthless.

Pinky Morris had been one of those men, or at least his late brother Frank was. Pinky was more of the Deputy Prime Minster, to cover the summer holidays. They arrived in S'aven, when it was still a town of tents and ramshackle buildings, to sell hooch and marijuana to the refugees. People were starving but they could all afford a couple of joints. Business grew rapidly and one day Pinky blinked and the Morris brothers were at the top of the pecking order with an entire city underneath them. Frank was the boss, all smiles and threats, and Pinky was always there to back his little brother up with brawn and attitude. Together they could do anything. And they did.

That was more than a decade ago, before Pinky lost his empire, lost his respect, lost his brother. He was about to turn fifty-five, he'd lost most of his hair, his stomach was starting to sag, and he was back to running a small drug cartel in the back of his wife's club like he was just approaching twenty. His life had circled and he was pinning everything he had on it starting again.

The walls of his office were plastered with photograph after photograph; a memorial to the good old days. The little frozen moments captured a time Pinky could barely believe had happened. Hundreds of historical faces stared at him from his cramped office at the back of the bar, scrutinising the state he was in. And why wouldn't they, they were from a time when he was on top and meant something in S'aven. Those glossy faces that surrounded him in his youth were gone now, mostly dead or hovering in the vicinity as haggard and as old and as spent as he was. What did they think of him now? It was a question he'd try to avoid asking himself. The answers only ever made him angry. After all it wasn't his fault he was fighting for space at the bottom of the sewers again; he was just a victim of circumstance.

But all of that was about to change. He could feel a ball vibrating in the pit of his stomach. It was ambition and it had been a long time since he'd allowed himself to dream. The depression was almost over.

His eyes fell on the face that occupied every single picture: his brother, Frank. Pinky had tried to change things when he died. He had to. Frank had left them penniless with a reputation as worthless as their bank balance. Pinky had watched Frank's demise, and he had decided to do things differently. He didn't want to rule the city in fear, watching his back in every reflection. He let things slide now and again. He let the Russians move closer to his territory. He went easy on his boys. And he watched as it all came apart. Frank would never have let it happen, Pinky could see that now. His brother wasn't perfect, but he was right for the city. S'aven needed a man like Frank Morris, and Pinky just regretted it had taken him seven sorry years to realise those shoes needed filling, not replacing.

The man sitting opposite him coughed, clearing his throat rather than trying to attract Pinky's attention. He used to be called Donnie Boom and his face was scattered across the wall beside nearly every picture of Frank, not that anyone would recognise him. Most of Donnie's face was melted away, scarred from the explosion seven years ago. Even Pinky had to second guess himself when Donnie first made contact again.

That was four months ago, and Donnie's grey eyeball still made Pinky's stomach churn. But even before the scars, Donnie was enough to give a grown man nightmares. Now he just looked like the monster he had always been inside. And after all this time apart Pinky had forgotten just how crazy his late brother's best friend actually was.

"You blew it up," Pinky stated with impatience. He rapped his fingers against the desk. His nails were bitten to the pinks of his fingers, the skin on his knuckles cracked and sore. They were the hands of an old man.

"I did what needed to be done."

"Under whose authority?"

Donnie eyed Pinky with intense frustration, that grey eyeball pulsating in its scorched socket. "Your brother's. That bitch killed him, she needed to be taught a lesson."

Pinky lifted his thick rimmed glasses and rubbed the tiredness from his eyes. Donnie didn't understand the situation in S'aven anymore, or he just didn't care. Blowing up the most reputable brothel in S'aven was like starting an underground war and he didn't have the man power or the money to fight it. He was beginning to regret allowing Donnie back into the fold despite all that Donnie was promising him.

"You need to lie low for a while."

"I can help with–"

Pinky raised his hand sharply. "You want to fucking help, you keep your bombs out of my city!" Pinky yelled, surprising himself.

He sat back in his chair and stared at Donnie. His temper was starting to get the better of him these days. He couldn't remember Frank ever yelling. He never had to; Frank commanded respect without it.

Pinky calmed himself and lowered his voice. "Enough buildings are going up around this place without you helping. People are going to be asking about you now, Donnie. My people are going to be asking about you."

"Then let them know I'm back. I don't get all this cloak and dagger shit."

"You don't get it. You put a bomb under my brother's table and blew him half way across S'aven!"

"I didn't mean to kill them. I told you, the instructions were from Frank's phone. I was set up."

"Exactly and you want the people who set you up on to us, do you? Whoever it was I want them with their guard down, do you understand me? You stay off the grid and don't come around here anymore. I'll call you when I need you."

"What about when you get the girl?"

"I'll call you. Once we have her, we have everything. But we have to play this carefully, Donnie. Frank pissed off a lot of people. We can't just assume it was Lulu Roxton that killed him. When we have the girl, we'll know."

Donnie nodded. He was crazy but he wasn't stupid.

"I appreciate what you're doing," he said running what was left of his hand through his matted red hair. "You didn't have to believe me."

"You took a risk coming back here, I figured you were either suicidal or telling the truth," Pinky told him.

"I had to," Donnie assured him. "I have to know who did it, Pinky. I loved Frank. What they made me do to him…" Donnie shook his head, close to crying – it was an unsettling sight. "You're right, I shouldn't be here. Sometimes it's hard for me to think. My head gets kind of messed up, from the explosion. I'll get out of your way."

He reached the door before he turned around. "You remember you said I'd get to finish them?"

Pinky nodded; he did remember. With that, Donnie left. There was no way Pinky was going to let some deranged, half mad pyromaniac finish anything.

"What did he want?" Pinky's wife stood in the open doorway.

"Revenge," Pinky replied.

Riva swayed into the room. For a woman in her forties she was still turning heads. She smiled at Pinky, it was a natural smile, unblemished by silicone and cosmetics like the rest of the wives he knew. Sometimes Pinky would look at her and wonder what the hell she was still doing with him. He wondered if she asked herself the same question.

"Any news on the girl?"

"They think they have her."

"Do you want me to send someone to get her?" The question set Pinky on edge. He still had men, not as many as the old days, but there was still an entourage. Only now his wife had her own money from the club and she was investing it all in a legal security firm which was making his own boys look like school kids. Using them would be better, but they were Riva's boys, Riva's bodyguards, Riva's heavies, Riva's assassins. Not his. He didn't like it.

Pinky shook his head. "I'm going to send a couple of the old guys." He didn't say 'my' guys for her benefit.

"What about those brothers?"

"We'll deal with them when she's safely locked away. This time it's going to be different, Riva. I'm going to get my city back."

4

Eight block towers bulged against the wilting greenery of Nelson Square. Each building a soaring twenty storeys of congested apartment spaces, squeezing families into single rooms with three foot square bathrooms and a water system that rivalled a third world country. Eight concrete hives, buzzing with an overzealous shot of electricity that flickered and shorted every time someone tried to boil a kettle. This was home for the people with jobs, where they could return for a few hours' sleep and be grateful they had a roof and a hundred other families over their heads. If safety came in numbers, this was the safest place on Earth.

Rachel's apartment was on the eleventh floor, not high enough to escape the smell, but, with the lift broken, it served as a free gym. She ran up the stairs, reached her door and struggled to unlock it in her panic. As she closed it, the second explosion shuddered through the room. The power cut out. Rachel stood in the dark and counted to ten. Nothing. She edged forward into the blackness, reaching for the bed, then the step up to the counter that pretended it was a kitchen. When she finally reached the sink she opened her curtains.

The power cut had taken out the whole square and the surrounding buildings. In the distance an orange glow marked the carnage she'd walked through. Blue lights flashed against the road; a strobe effect for the siren disco shrilling through the night. It gave her just enough light to make out the rest of her apartment. Not that there was much to see. The bed, the kitchen area, a chest of drawers and her boyfriend's pride and joy: the battered old television. The lights suddenly flickered back on. The electricity board was getting quicker at sorting out the shortages, but then they were having to do it four or five times a day.

Her head was throbbing. She massaged her temples and felt a gash in her forehead. It wasn't deep but she'd been face down in whatever shit had built up on the road. If she didn't clean it there'd be a cardboard box and incinerator with her name on it. She ran through her chores as she made her way to the shower room. She needed to wash, to eat, and to sleep. She desperately needed to sleep.

Her private time was regimented like a military operation. She showered under a trickle of icy water in the dark, washing away the blood and rubble. Ignoring the shivers, she dressed herself in as many layers as she could find and searched the kitchen until she found her supply of protein bars. She ate a single bar on the bed, chewing it into a manageable paste and washing it down with half a cup of the stale water she had boiled before her shift started. It had taken her twenty minutes, leaving her just over five and a half hours for sleep.

It didn't matter what had happened. Instinct claimed her body and she wrapped herself up in the duvets. Her eyes dropped before her head hit the pillow and for the final moments of consciousness all she could see was the stranger's face. He was nothing like what she had expected, looking more like a male model than a peeping tom. The weight of his hand still pressed into her shoulder, protecting her or controlling her, it was hard to tell.

"Rach', are you awake?"

Something clattered onto the floor–it sounded like dishes. She blinked in the dull light while her hand patted the floor to find the small alarm clock under the bed. Three hours sleep – just great. She groaned and sat up, there was no point trying for a fourth. Mark was rummaging through the cupboards, trying to be as quiet as he could and failing miserably.

She sat up and watched him creaking open the cupboards, shuffling their pans around in an idle, fruitless search until he found the tin of protein bars which she always kept on the same shelf, in the same cupboard. Four years and he still couldn't remember–four long, miserable years.

"Hey, you're awake!" It was a mixture of surprise and delight, Mark's default mood. He was always happy, always smiling like a simpleton while the world around him fell apart.

Rachel couldn't repay the sentiment.

"I am now," she grumbled. "Are you still on duty?"

Usually Mark changed at the police station. She rarely saw him in full uniform–a *status quo* she preferred. There was something about it–the armour, the badge, something about the whole persona of a cop that turned her stomach. Mark wasn't a bad looking guy but in his padding and helmet he was repulsive. Cops were different in S'aven. They didn't solve crime, they didn't keep the streets safe. Cops in S'aven made sure nothing bad got into the city and nothing good got out. "Protect and Serve" was embroidered into every jacket; they just overlooked the "Ourselves" clause to their oath.

"Yeah, there was this big explosion–did you hear it?"

Lying to him came more naturally than telling the truth. "No, must have slept through."

"It's bad. Really bad. Seven dead. Can you believe it?"

Seven? That couldn't be right. There had been so many bodies wedged under that rubble with their arms and legs poking out in a gruesome game of lucky dip. She stared at Mark totally confused, then she realised; he was talking about cops. All cops care about are other cops. Dead vagrants are as good as litter; blow them to pieces and they're easier to clean up. But cops, well they're as precious as gold in the city, never mind that most of them are dirtier than S'aven's mob cartels.

"Do you know who was responsible?"

"Terrorists."

It was always terrorists. Hundreds of anti-government groups in S'aven alone and they're all lumped together as terrorists. The city would broadcast what to look for: foreigners, dark skinned, religious. They could be Muslims, Jews, Sikhs, even the white Catholics were *the enemy*. The fact they'd just as well blow each other up along with the police didn't matter. The government didn't negotiate with terrorists, no matter how many families were scattered in bite-sized pieces across the slums.

Rachel shook her head; there was no point reasoning with Mark. He believed what the Sergeant told him and he'd uphold his beliefs until someone bludgeoned his thick skull. Sometimes she wondered if that someone would be her. Sometimes she fantasised about it.

"Gary will be here in a minute," Mark said as he crammed a protein bar into his mouth.

"What? Why?"

Cops made her uneasy, but Mark's partner Gary made her skin crawl. London's police force reclaimed their position as law enforcers from the army more than two decades ago when the worst of the country's troubles had passed.

But the boys in blue were easily susceptible to bribery and corruption. Most cops were just hired thugs in uniform who roamed their beats, happily abusing their power and authority. Scotland Yard was under direct control from the government, the only body more corrupt than London's hand of justice. But the surplus police force that took watch over S'aven and other backwater towns were generally ignored by Parliament and instead were on the payroll of the gang lords that controlled the territories. If there was ever a caricature for how bad the police could actually be it was PC Gary Willis; the poster child for all things wrong with S'aven's law enforcement.

"He had something he needed to sort out. We were supposed to be first on the scene, Sarge is going to want to know why we weren't there. We need to get our stories straight."

It was only then Rachel realised that the second explosion was intended for him. If he'd been doing his job properly his body would be one of the seven and she'd still be asleep. It was a strange thought.

"Why weren't you there?" She asked before her mind started to run away.

"I was running the patrol as normal, but couldn't show up without Gary. They'd haul his ass up for investigation. He's already on two strikes."

There was no point asking where Gary was, Mark wouldn't know and Rachel could take too many unpleasant guesses.

"You're going to get three strikes if this keeps going on, never mind Gary."

"I'll be fine. It's not like the hospital, Rach', we look out for each other. It's cool." He turned to her and frowned. "Hey, what happened to your head?"

He sat beside her and brushed the dark strands of hair from her eyes. She felt a pang of guilt. He didn't deserve to be splattered over the street with the rest of his colleagues.

"I tripped at work. It's nothing. I just need to sleep."

This time he got the hint.

"I'll go meet Gary outside, let you get some rest. Starting your shift soon?"

"A few hours."

"I guess I'll see you on my way out tomorrow then." He kissed her tenderly. Beneath the suit, the ignorance and the lack of common sense, he wasn't a bad guy. Not like his partner.

A pounding on the door interrupted them. Rachel sighed, she could already feel her body tensing. Mark gave her a sheepish shrug.

"Open up, it's the police!" It was Gary, and he sounded drunk.

"Sorry," he murmured.

"You'd better let him in before he wakes the entire floor."

Mark had barely got the lock turned when the door was shoved open. His partner's first step into the room was edgy; he was more than drunk. Then his eyes fell on Rachel. Cracking his acne-covered face into a smile he leered at her. She was wearing four layers, sitting underneath three duvets, but the gesture still made her feel naked. She pulled the covers over her exposed neck and shied back towards the wall. Gary frightened her and he took great enjoyment in doing it.

"Sorry, was I interrupting?"

"No, I just need to take a leak. Give me a minute and we can go," Mark said as he rushed to the shower room. He was oblivious to how Rachel felt about his partner. She wondered, if he knew, what he would have done about it.

"So Rachel, Rachel, Rachel," he said, approaching the bed with more confidence than Mark had ever mustered. "Sweet dreams?"

"You're going to get Mark sacked if you keep letting him cover for you."

"Hey, my partner is a team player–can't help that. Don't worry, if anything happens to him I can always put a roof over your head. For a price." His fat fingers reached for the duvet.

The toilet flushed. He'd let go by the time Mark returned.

"Okay, here's my notebook for you to copy. Let's go." Mark gave her a brief kiss on the top of her head and ushered his partner towards the door. Rachel had to take another shower before she could settle.

5

Cold mornings were the worst. Charlie woke early, feeling the agony ringing through his body; his very own malicious alarm clock. He lay on the bed, unable to move his legs without crying out. John was on the floor, resting calmly on his back, as though there was nowhere else in the world more comfortable. His eyes were closed, but Charlie couldn't work out if he was still asleep or just waiting – he did that sometimes. Either way Charlie couldn't risk taking his final pills in the same room. The last thing he needed was John finding out everything.

When the pain had dulled and the ache in his bladder worsened he found the energy to haul himself up. With the crutch bearing most of the effort, he made it to the bathroom and swallowed his last pills dry before relieving himself. Immediately his head started to ease, his thoughts slurred slightly, but it was better than the pain. Anything was better than the morning pain.

He turned to wash his hands and looked down at the orange stained sink. With the aches temporarily subdued he could work on his powers. Letting his hand hover over the tap, he concentrated. His temples began to burn with the effort. His hand trembled, but slowly the tap turned. Water trickled and then flooded out. Compared to what he had been it was pathetic, but the past year had been an endless struggle and this, at last, was an improvement.

He left the bathroom with a smile. John was already up, sitting at the table and going through the file as though he'd been there all night. His fingers loitered on the folded sheet of torn paper. It was the remains of a letter, written seven years ago by the girl in the opposite tower. It didn't say much, just that she had work in a hospital, she would start in a week – a week seven years ago – and it was signed: *R*.

"Do I even want to know?" John said without even looking at his brother's smirk.

"I turned the tap on," Charlie announced proudly.

John put the letter down and gave his elder brother an incredulous stare. "Good for you," he eventually replied in a voice rich with sarcasm. "I boiled the kettle, together who knows what we could do."

"I mean, smart ass, I turned the tap on hands-free."

John's unimpressed expression wavered slightly. "Not bad," he replied, but they both knew for a man who had once driven a car whilst locked in the boot, it was far from astounding. "See what happens when you get your head back in the game."

The mobile on the table started ringing. John nudged it towards Charlie, he didn't like phones – or people for that matter.

"It's him."

Charlie carefully picked it up, trying not to let it see how nervous he really was. He could do this – he could play the game. He had to.

"Mr Morris, good to hear from you."

"Do you have what I asked for?" Pinky Morris asked.

"We agreed we'd be done by two and we will. And I am confident you'll be very satisfied."

"You're sure it's her?"

"We've got one last 't' to cross and we'll be done. But I can tell you there's no doubt in my mind it's her."

"Don't be late." He made way for the dial tone.

Charlie stared at the phone. "I don't like that guy."

The explosion had taken out the top windows of St Mary's Hospital. A riot six months earlier had already claimed the lower floors. From the entrance the building looked as desolate as those around it; boards nailed to every surface, decorated in anti-everything graffiti and weathering with the brickwork. If hell had a gate it looked just like the entrance to St Mary's.

The outside of the hospital did little to prepare Charlie for the inside. The explosion victims were still piling in from the surrounding rubble. What was left of the serious injuries was awaiting identification in the morgue. Charlie squeezed himself into the manic reception room. He reached for his wallet and headed for the front desk, which was really just a sealed cage protecting the nurses inside. His eyes flicked around the emergency room. There was no sign of Rachel.

He didn't need to see her up close. He didn't need to visit her work, or do any more investigation to complete the job. She was the girl they were looking for. He was sure of it. What he did need was a prescription and a hospital like St Mary's was a perfect cover for getting one without John knowing. If Rachel stayed out of his way all the better.

He walked up to the reception nurse. She looked tired, but then every white coat in the building looked tired. She banged her computer monitor as he approached and settled back down into her worn seat behind the mesh frame encasing her desk. The hospital supplemented most of its income from private sales, there should have been no reason Charlie's purchase would cause a problem. If anything they would be grateful for his custom.

"Morning," he said with a forced grin.

"Name?"

"Sorry?"

"Your name?"

"Eh, I'm just after a prescription." He withdrew his wallet, flashing her sight of the notes he was willing to part with to speed her up.

It was then she gave him her full, unimpressed attention. "Pharmacy stocks are running low. Emergency prescriptions only until Tuesday. If you need the pills you give me your name and a doctor will see you and sign off on any drugs you need."

"Seriously?"

She gave him a self-satisfied smile. "Name?"

"David Jones," he replied, it was the name on his empty pill bottle.

"Have a seat Mr. Jones, someone will call you shortly."

There were eight seats in the reception room and forty people wedging themselves into clusters on the dust covered floor. Charlie decided to stand to avoid the possibility of disease. The outbreaks in S'aven came mercilessly fast. When the poor got sick they crammed themselves into hospital waiting rooms to share their bacteria. You were more likely to catch something in St Mary's than crawling around on your belly in the sewers.

That morning at least the waiting room seemed to be populated with open wounds and broken bones, forcing anyone with a raised temperature to wait outside in the cold. He scanned the faces carefully, checking for discolouration, pigmented eyes, any signs of N-strain or worse. Then he noticed, sandwiched between a man with a towel pressed against his bloody face and a woman with a glass shard as big as her fist wedged into her leg, a kid sweating like he was in a furnace. His body twitched impatiently, jumping at the sight of every nurse walking by. Charlie had seen kids like that growing up all over the city, hooked on a local blend, caught up in crime and left stranded when they were no longer useful. It was a short, tragic life. The length of his future was down to luck, whether it be days or weeks – never longer.

Charlie wiped the sweat from his forehead and fidgeted and jumped when the man standing in front of him got up to leave. Patients were called, more piled in. Soon the open wounds were replaced with the split stitches and infections as the rotation of injuries aged. Charlie watched the doctors passing through, shouting out name after name. He never caught sight of Rachel.

He was considering braving the floor, when a commotion broke out. The drug addict was getting restless. The people around him had been called already, but he still sat there, going cold turkey. Paranoia fuelled him and he just flipped. Charlie watched as the muttering grew into shouting, than as the shouting grew louder. He screamed at the nurse trying to calm him down. Then he pushed her. Another nurse rushed to the commotion, but he had lost control. He grabbed her and attempted to hit her hard in the face.

Charlie flinched, but the punch never happened. Standing behind him, hand on his shoulder was Rachel. Slowly, the kid let go of the nurse. He turned around and stared at Rachel. Charlie peered closer. The kid wasn't staring at all, he was listening. Only Rachel's mouth wasn't saying anything. The kid nodded, shrugged and left.

Charlie swallowed. His senses were tingling. She was a Reacher. He stared at her suddenly feeling the fool. He realised now he should have asked why Pinky was so desperate to uncover this simple doctor. He should have dug a little deeper and found out more about the girl. He should have found out more about Pinky. All these regrets rolled around in his head until they settled on the one fact he could cling to. She was a Reacher, just like him.

And that changed everything.

6

She was a Reacher and she was still alive.

She had lived in S'aven for seven years, sharing a house with a cop, and she was still alive.

Charlie couldn't understand it. Reachers had to keep running, settling anywhere for long was too dangerous. He learned that from his own tragic experience. You never knew when the patrols would come for you. All it would take was one suspicious neighbour, or somebody with a grudge, and they were carting you off for the good of humanity. It didn't matter if you were male, female, young or old–the only way to escape was to run. One year, two months, and nine days ago they had come for him, taking his daughter, an innocent child, but still a Reacher in the eyes of the government. As soon as you settled it was too late. But somehow Rachel had stayed in the same city, the same apartment, the same job, and she was still using her powers. He was in awe of her and at the same time overwhelmed with the idea of shaking her and telling her to get out before she was spotted.

He could see her clearly now, bringing in patients with the other doctors, and he realised that was how she had stayed hidden: it was her talent, her Reacher skill. He could turn on taps with his mind and she could make herself seemingly invisible in a room full of people. Somehow she had been there all along and he had just been unable to see her. Only now he knew this. There she was, as vibrant as the blood spatter up the wall. Only now he wasn't the only one who was looking for her. He thought back to the day his daughter was taken and his whole chest started to hurt; he couldn't let that happen again.

They needed the job and the money, but Charlie couldn't give another Reacher up. There was a code, one he lived his life by, about protecting his own kind. But it was more than that. He'd been to the laboratories; he knew what happened to those born with powers, those they called Reachers, psychics, plague-bringers. You could get a big pay-out if you found one. Was that the reason Pinky wanted her? Charlie swallowed. How could he hand her over, risk her being dragged off to spend the rest of her life in an empty white cell, with electrode burns over her body? He couldn't, but he'd already told Pinky that he had her.

"David Jones!"

He had to tell John. His head was all over the place, but John would be able to think straight. He'd know what to do.

"David Jones!"

It should have been a simple job. Father Darcy had promised them a simple job. Why couldn't it have been a simple job?

"Last call for David Jones!"

Charlie paused and looked at the doctor shouting his alias. He wasn't even surprised it was Rachel calling his name. With the way his luck was going he half expected John to be waiting at the door, watching the whole sorry affair unfold.

"Sorry, that's me," he said sheepishly.

"Good. You nearly missed your turn there, Mr. Jones. Come on, I don't bite."

She led the way through the terrace of closed curtains and muffled cries, until she reached an empty bed, with a disinfected plastic sheet over it.

"Hop yourself up Mr. Jones, I'll just get the paperwork."

"Actually I just came in for a prescription," Charlie started, holding out his bottle like a beggar.

"Well you're in luck, today we're giving free examinations with every bottle of pills. I'll be two seconds, don't you go away." She swiped the bottle from him, probably to check his non-existent record.

Charlie scowled to himself. She was a good doctor. Things were going from dire to disastrous.

She returned with a professional, knowing smile. He'd been tracking her for two weeks but this was the first time he had seen her in the flesh. Her photograph had made her look older, but up close he could see the city hadn't totally robbed her of her youth. And she was sharp too; he could tell that just from her eyes. There would be no chance of getting one over on her and she wouldn't appreciate him trying.

Charlie realised he was staring. He turned away and tried to decide what he was going to do. If her powers were stronger than his she might be able to read his thoughts, and then there'd be nowhere to hide. He had to think quickly, but his mind went blank.

"So, repeat prescription is it, for the leg?"

"Eh, no, it's for my back."

Her pencil tapped against her clipboard. "And what's happened to your back?"

"It's an old wound, happened a year ago." *One year, two months, and nine days to be exact*, he thought to himself. "Nerve damage." He didn't like talking about it, especially to her.

"I see, and you're still getting pain?"

"Yeah."

"What are we talking here, bad pain, sharp twinges, rolling on the floor in agony?"

"Very bad pain."

Rachel sat on the bed beside him. He'd never been good at the mind reading side of his powers, sure he could have lifted her into the air back in the day, but he would have no idea what was going on in her head.

"Would you mind if I took a peek, make sure all's healing well?"

"There's no point, I just need the prescription." He tried to squirm away from her. If she wasn't strong enough to read him from a distance, touching him would probably do the trick.

"If it's an old wound and it's still giving you so much trouble that you have to take a daily morphine pill, I need to make sure everything is okay."

She had his shirt up before he could protest further. Charlie slumped forward, feeling like a child getting ready for his jabs. She had a way about her. It was forceful but at the same time friendly. Her hands hovered over his skin. She wasn't wearing gloves, probably due to cutbacks, so she was trying to avoid making skin contact.

"A knife wound," she stated. "Stabbed three times, nasty. Healed up nicely though. You must have had a good surgeon. But I'm thinking, given you're still on medication, that you didn't bother with the aftercare." She pulled his shirt back down and stood with an air of empathy about her.

He sighed. She didn't suspect he was a Reacher, just another useless junkie after a fix. Relief almost set in and then he realised she was going to have to know the truth – the whole truth. She was a Reacher, he couldn't just leave her to her fate.

"I take it you didn't get any counselling?"

"My budget only ran to the surgeon."

"Well if you've got to spend your money you might as well get stitched up first."

"There's not much point getting follow up care if I'm dead."

"Exactly. I'm going to level with you Mr. Jones. You know as well as I do the medication you're taking is way too strong for an injury like yours. The pain you're in is likely to be psychosomatic…"

Charlie put up his hands. He had to do something. "A lecture isn't necessary. Listen I need to talk to you."

"Okay, if that's what you want." Her smile stayed, but her eyes betrayed her unease.

She was going to read him, or press a thought into his head. Then it would be over. He had to act now. He needed money, so much so he was contemplating leaving her in Pinky Morris's hands, but he couldn't do it. He'd lost nearly everything in his life–giving away his morality would finish him.

"You need to get out of the city tonight," he said quickly.

Her smile faltered. "I'm sorry?"

"I know what you are," he whispered.

She started backing away. Charlie jumped off the bed, meaning to stop her but his leg buckled. He fell into her and was amazed she managed to catch him and help him back to the bed.

"It's okay," he assured her. "You're safe. We're the same. I'm not going to tell anyone."

She didn't believe him and why would she? Reachers were rare and getting rarer. Charlie hadn't seen another one in years, apart from his daughter. But then her senses got the better of her and she could feel, just like he could, that bond that only exists between their kind. It was like coming home, a warm comfortable sigh in the bottom of your stomach.

"If you're not going to tell anyone why do I have to leave the city?"

"Because people are looking for you already. You won't be able to hide here anymore. Not now that they're looking. I have to go," Charlie said.

"Wait–you just came here to tell me to leave?"

"Actually I came for my prescription. If you don't mind."

Her face tightened and she looked like she was about to argue, to try to convince him that popping pills wasn't going to solve anything, but the longer they were together the less time she had to get to safety.

"You still want the drugs, even though they're causing you more harm than good?"

He shrugged, feeling even more pathetic than usual. "I can pay."

"I shouldn't give it to you." Shaking her head she handed him his prescription. Their hands brushed and they both felt the connection surge. Charlie closed his eyes; the familiarity between them was instantaneous, as though their powers were magnetic. The urge to protect her would just get stronger, and she was probably feeling the same for him. He had to push his instincts aside if he was going to make it out of the hospital.

He put his pills in his pocket and dared to glance at her one more time. She was so young, but already the world was taking its toll. He'd warned her, but that would never be enough. Eventually she would stop running and they would catch her. She would die alone; they always did. Taking his crutch he left her at the bed, feeling like a coward.

He found John three streets down from the hospital, eyeballing the car that was trying to reverse park in front of their rented vehicle. If John had the power the driver's head would have exploded already. Charlie got into the passenger seat and assessed John's mood. His younger brother was clenching the steering wheel so tightly his knuckles were going blue. Charlie sighed, it couldn't get any worse.

"We've got a problem," Charlie began.

John turned his head, and if his eyes kept darting back at the offending driver, Charlie ignored it.

"She's a Reacher. I guess that explains why they want her."

John scowled. "They hired you, why would they want her?"

"I'm not sure."

John's fingers rapped against the wheel. "A Reacher ... that complicates things. Gives you one hell of a moral issue too. What do you want to do?"

Charlie pursed his lips awkwardly. "I may have told her to get out of the city."

"I see," John was using his restrained *I'm trying to suppress the urge to kill you* voice. "So you made contact with her?"

"Only after you did, asshole."

John wasn't laughing. "And you told her?"

"I was unspecific. I said she was in danger and she had to leave."

"Okay, so when we meet Pinky in," he checked his watch, "forty minutes, what are we going to do?"

Charlie folded his arms. "I'll think of something. Always do, don't I?"

"We're not going to get paid, are we?"

"We'll get paid, I promise."

"We're not going to get paid," John groaned.

"John, listen to me, man, we will get paid. And if we don't I'll give you my share." Charlie winked.

John started the car, grumbling to himself. "First shitty job we do and we don't even get paid for it."

Charlie decided to ignore him. He had forty minutes to come up with something. As long as Rachel was moving she would have enough time to get out of the city. He just hoped she was as smart as she looked.

7

The night before a bullet tore through her father's back he had sat Rachel down with her sister Isobel.

She was six years old, it was snowing and they were never going to see home again. He told them both about the running game. It was a game of strategy – to stay alive you needed to know when to run and where. Every room, every house, every city had its exits, each taking time, each with their own set of obstacles. To win you needed to pick the best escape route. The prize – you got to stay alive.

Rachel had got complacent, she'd allowed herself to settle, to let her guard down, used her powers in front of others, but she had never stopped playing the game. She was scared – it was a game of luck as much as skill – but she kept a cool head. As casually as she could manage she walked through the hospital, her pace no different from the rest of the staff hurrying to keep people out of the morgue. She slipped by them unnoticed, made her way to her locker, grabbed her bag and headed for the fire exit.

The bitter air slapped her face, reminding her of the winter threatening the city. She could run now, head out of the city on foot, make it to the country in a couple of hours, but with no food, no money, how long would she last? Charlie had given her time and if she wanted to live she had to use it wisely. That was how to play the game properly – never panic, always think one step ahead.

The side exit backed on to an alleyway cutting a path towards the open market. She hurried, her feet smashing puddles of trash and slurry into her trouser legs. The buildings around her, concrete coffins from another century, started to fall away and the first open market shacks came into view. Dubious meat hung from poles around her, circled by flies and hungrier children. The crowd was heavy and lazy, scrutinising and succumbing to the array of oddities the tradespeople procured. This was S'aven as it had been at the start – a shanty town bazaar, built up of tin shacks and cobbled together houses. Over the years the city had grown, but the market had never changed – some things just don't.

Rachel put her head down and slipped through the masses unseen. There were cops up ahead, they circled the market like carrion birds, picking up what they could with a flick of their badge. There were always more men in blue at the start of the week when the produce was fresh, but supplies were starting to dwindle, leaving the runts of the force picking up the scraps. She passed by the two of them, they didn't give her a second glance.

The market abruptly finished at the edge of the canal. Children swarmed the waterway, poking at the slurry ditch, looking for bodies. The autumn sun seemed to focus all its efforts here, sweating the layers of shit and putrefying the air around. Rachel held her breath and quickened her pace.

The city was getting dirtier, it was growing in size but not in space. Another square of columns was being mashed together from the offcuts of another of London's architectural wonders. Towers of houses littered the skyline, obliterating the horizon and the world beyond.

S'aven wasn't London, it wasn't anything more than a consolation prize for the poverty stricken, but for four years it had been Rachel's home. She marvelled at it now as though she were arriving for the first time. It had delivered its promise to her, it had been her safe haven since the moment she had arrived. She found a job, a flat, it was more than most. When she left it would be gone. She had no papers, no credentials she could rely on. Once her feet crossed the border she would never be able to return. The thought weighed heavily.

Rachel turned the corner, reaching Nelson Square. She stared up at her tower block. *They* could be waiting for her, watching for her. She had to move quickly, her thoughts racing with the rest of her.

The north of the country was barren and impenetrable in the winter. If the snow hadn't arrived it would be on its way. Even if she could find somewhere safe to stay in time, there were still guerrilla gangs moving into the towns up there, commandeering their own little piece of England.

The door to her building was clear. She took the stairs two at a time, then ran through her corridor until she reached the front door.

The south was where the money was. Sandy beaches in summer, turbine powered heating in the winter. The only thing between her and a retirement in the sun was a couple grand and some authentic identity papers. She dismissed the idea altogether. The law enforcement was sharper down there and on the lookout for her kind.

She opened the door and stopped in her tracks. Mark was asleep on the bed. He started to stir. She reached out and touched his head, letting her fingers massage his skull.

"Sleep," she commanded and waited for him to settle back down. He started to snore.

It left the west. If she kept to the countryside she might make it as far as Wales, head southbound and find a small hospital willing to take her on. She could lie low there, let the winter pass and move on in the spring. It wasn't great, but it was the winning play.

She stripped off her scrubs, pulled on her best trousers, a thermal vest and sweater. She had to travel light – if she couldn't wear it she would leave it behind. Under the sink, in an old bleach bottle, was three hundred pounds in used notes. She stuffed the money into her bra and grabbed her empty rucksack. She filled the rucksack with as many protein bars as she could carry, clean underwear and a bar of soap, then headed out of the door.

As it closed she paused. This would be the last time she would see Mark. They'd been together a long time and, although they weren't the best years of her life, he was still a good man. He'd be so lost without her too. Would he try to find her? Probably, but he wouldn't succeed. And then what? Would he find someone else or would the heartache be too much? He loved her deeply and, even though she didn't feel the same, she didn't want to hurt him. But what choice did she have? If they found her she was as good as dead anyway. At least this way he had a chance to move on. She pressed her hand against the door apologetically and then continued down the corridor.

There was no point leaving him a note, there was nothing she could say that he would ever understand.

8

The Cage was S'aven's hotspot. Anyone with any money spent it on the cage fights or at the tables, night after night. The bar was owned by Pinky's wife, but the undercurrent of crime happening in the back office was all Pinky's. It wasn't much of an empire, nothing compared to what it had been when Frank Morris was working his magic, but there were rumours that it was growing.

The club was closed, but the door was wide open. Two women scrubbed at vomit stains splattered over the door frame. They spared Charlie and John nothing more than a glance. It was a common sight to see men like them. There were no windows inside the building and most of the lights were off. Charlie could just about make out the edge of the cage that drew in the punters and of course the bar, which was lit up like a welcoming beacon.

A woman in her late forties toyed with a stock list, watching them approach without looking up. In her day she had been a stunner and even now she could outshine most women twenty years her junior. As they reached the bar she lifted her head and beamed at them. It was infectious. Charlie grinned back. John was immune.

"Let me guess, the infamous Smith brothers." She held out her manicured hand and shook Charlie's. "I'm Pinky's wife. It's nice to meet you boys, I've heard a lot about you. Pinky's just finishing up some business and he'll be right with you. Can I get you boys something to drink? We've got the real stuff here."

"Thanks, we're good. Nice place you've got here Mrs Morris," Charlie lied.

"Call me Riva, Mrs Morris was my mother-in-law – it's not a flattering comparison. You sure I can't fix you up something? I used to be a mean cocktail waitress in my day."

There was a side door behind the bar. It opened as Pinky's meeting finished. Charlie recognised some of the faces from years gone by. It was funny, their skin wrinkled, their hair fell out, but the clothes stayed the same. He picked out Pablo immediately, he was Pinky's right hand and as old school as they came, still wearing the same green fedora he had when he used to work Frank Morris' girls on the streets. Behind him was Fat Joe – the money man – in a white shirt stained with pasta sauce, as classy as he had ever been. They walked out with a younger guy, one Charlie didn't recognise. He walked with a swagger, eyeballing Charlie and John as he passed as though he could easily take them out.

Then came Pinky. He had the body of frail old man, but there was nothing diminishing about him. His wiry arms were still strong. Beneath his thick rimmed glasses his eyes were still sharp. And the yellow cardigan he was wearing was concealing his fully armed gun holster. He didn't acknowledge Charlie or John but with a flick of his head gestured for them to follow him.

"You got a plan yet?" John murmured under his breath.

Charlie didn't. "Of course I do."

The room was brightly lit, with each wall shining a light on a memorial of the Morris family history. Charlie scanned his eyes quickly across the pictures. So many faces, so many judgemental eyes, Charlie wondered how a man could stay sane in such a strong shadow of his past. They were offered a seat and it was straight to business. Pinky secured himself behind his desk and pressed his hands together, gathering control of the room in the tips of his fingers.

"You boys got good news for me."

John removed the file from his bag and pushed it across the desk.

"Rachel Aaron, twenty-four, doctor at St Mary's. We've got her current address, she's got no other places in the city she's likely to be. We've included her work schedule and the routes she usually takes. I've verified her personally. She's the girl who wrote the letter," Charlie assured him.

"All of this in just two weeks." Pinky was unconvinced.

"We're very good at what we do." Charlie leaned forward, trying to be as friendly as possible, playing the only card he could. "One complication I should tell you about though. Her boyfriend's a cop, and they share the apartment. We found her in two weeks but we didn't have time to run any checks on him–just a name. Now if you want to give us another week I can get you a whole second file. If you think you need it, that is." And that was his plan, to play for more time.

The Running Game

Pinky looked to be considering it. He rested forward on the file and examined his guests. "I like you boys. And this is good work. If all my men were like you I'd still have hair on my head. You boys have talent, talent I could use. I could put a lot more work your way, if you're interested."

There was a pause. A dangerous pause.

Charlie cleared his throat. "Certainly something we'd consider Pinky," he lied. "If the money's right." But it wouldn't be right. All Charlie wanted was the cash they were owed and they would be out of S'aven before sunset – he hoped Rachel would be doing the same.

"Well boys, if you want to come back tomorrow I'll have your money for you, maybe even another job."

"Tomorrow!" Charlie exclaimed. "We were under the impression we'd be paid today, given we've handed over everything. You know, on time, as instructed."

Pinky shifted in his seat, ensuring what little weight he had was evenly thrown around the room. "I've got an old priest's word that you two are the real deal. You've come up with a name when six other guys failed. And you did that in two weeks. When your work pays off so will I. After that consider your trust earned and your name in this city to be worth gold. Can't say fairer than that."

Charlie sat back and dared a glance in John's direction. The younger Smith was even less amused.

"That's not how we do business," John said and the mood in the room shifted.

"This isn't up for negotiation, son. You want to keep on my good side, and believe me you do, you'll humour me."

John was furious. Charlie quickly interjected, "So we come back tomorrow and we get the price we agreed?"

"Same time tomorrow and you walk away with the cash you deserve. I appreciate your patience Charlie. You boys get yourselves a couple of drinks tonight, on the house."

Their cue to leave was underlined in his tone. And despite the handshake there was nothing amicable about their meeting. Pinky had them over a barrel and there was nothing Charlie could do about it.

They left the club in silence. John unlocked the car, claimed the driver's seat, and waited for his brother. Charlie closed his door and waited. And waited. And waited. Until eventually his brother broke the silence.

"So the plan, did it work?" John sneered.

"What do you think?"

Charlie's head was pounding so hard he had to close his eyes. His fingertips danced on the hem of his pocket. Inside his pills were calling to him, promising to take the edge off and make the world bearable again. He thought about just taking one subtly. Slowly his fingers slipped inside his pocket and his phone snapped at him.

He fished it out. "Dad" flashed up on the screen. Charlie sighed and took the call.

"Darcy," he groaned, adding another notch to his bad day.

"Hey Charlie, just checking everything went okay. You get the job done?"

"Not really. We've got a problem."

"That sounds ominous. John didn't upset Pinky did he?"

"No, John was on his best behaviour." Charlie ignored the look he got from his brother. "Turns out the mark is a Reacher."

Darcy didn't say anything.

"And I told her she was in trouble and that she should get out of the city."

"What did you say to Pinky?"

"Nothing, just handed him the file, only now the bastard won't pay us until he gets his pay off, which probably means we're not going to get our money."

"You gave him a Reacher's file!" Darcy's outrage came as no surprise.

"What else could I do? If she's smart she'll have disappeared already."

"Only now he has her picture and a breadcrumb trail. Charlie this is serious. She could be in real danger."

"So what am I supposed to do?"

"You get that girl and you bring her to me."

"I thought you were retired."

"You don't retire from helping God's people. Get her to me Charlie, I still have contacts in convents in the south, I'll see her safe. Can you do this?"

"What about the money?"

"This is more important than money."

He hung up the phone as John pulled up the car.

"So it looks like we're going to save Rachel," Charlie explained and rubbed his temples rigorously.

"What if she's already left the city?"

"She can't move that fast on foot. She'll have gone to the train station. Not the closest one to her." He clicked his fingers. "Trinity, she could walk there quick enough. She won't have the money to go south, north is out with the winter coming. She'll be westbound."

John pulled back onto the road. "What if you're wrong?"

"When have I ever been wrong?"

"Do you want the list?"

"Fine, drop me off. You head to the hospital, then her flat, make sure she isn't there and keep an eye out for Pinky's boys. We don't want them thinking we're involved in her disappearance."

9

The afternoon daylight whipped at Roxy's eyes. His tuxedo was scarred with debauchery and torn at the sleeve. He scratched at his mop of yellow hair and scanned the bleary faces around him. Despite the hangover, the vomit stains over his trousers, and his missing socks, it had been a very profitable night. He was poor of pocket but rich with information. He fished out a packet of liquorice cigarettes and ran one under his nose. Breakfast; the most important smoke of the day.

He checked his phone as he meandered down the street, looking for an update from his beloved mother as she recovered in hospital. The burns to her arms and legs weren't as bad as some of her girls, but broken pride was difficult to mend. She'd left him just one message, some filth about one of her doctors. Roxy sent a quick text back, telling her he was close.

It wasn't his usual line of work, but his play at being a detective had paid off. A few days poking in the right places had spooked out the identity of the bastard who planted the bomb on his mother's doorstep and once he knew the man the rest of the plot fell into place.

Donnie Boom had been a name from the past. By the time Roxy took to the strip the Scotsman was an urban legend; the man who had taken down Frank Morris and then disappeared into the sunset. Only now he was back, or at least he was rumoured to be. And the mad Scotsman was scratching at old wounds again, stirring up the forgotten history between his dear old mum and the Morris family.

Seven years had done a lot to suppress the tension between Lulu Roxton and Pinky Morris. The feud was long over, or at least it had been until Donnie Boom started living up to his namesake again. Now Roxy's mum was laid up in

The Running Game

a hospital bed and somebody was going to have to pay. One way or the other Donnie was going to pay. The only thing Roxy didn't know: who was Donnie working for?

He skipped through the traffic on his way to Pinky's club. All he needed was the go-ahead from Pinky and the status quo would resume. And why wouldn't Pinky authorise the killing? Donnie had blown up his brother after all, hell he'd probably pay Roxy to do it.

Roxy turned the corner and stopped mid-step. He couldn't believe it. Two men were walking out of the club. Two men that he never expected to see in S'aven again. Roxy sidled back into the shadows and watched the Smith brothers leave. An unusual stirring of emotion started to build in him. It had been just over a year since he'd last been in the company of his old team and the taste in the back of his mouth was still bitter. There were no coincidences in this world, only opportunities and if the Smiths were back then he might just be in luck.

He waited until their car turned off and resumed his swagger. He didn't have an appointment, but he knew Pinky would be expecting him to drop by at some point. He took the main entrance to the club, greeting the staff as though he owned them. Everyone knew Roxy; the penniless, the millionaires, he was everybody's friend, until of course he ripped you off.

Pinky's boys were clustered around a table counting the takings in front of the empty cage. Roxy smiled to himself, *Pinky's boys* – they were all old enough to be his father. And any one of them could be. Fat Joe noticed him first. He nodded, wobbling the jowls of flab dangling from his face. With that the others stopped counting the wads of cash.

Joe wheezed, about to stand up. He was Pinky's bookkeeper, the Morris money man and Pinky's cousin on his mother's side. His business was Pinky's money and the mere sight of Roxy's sticky fingers made him more than nervous.

"What do you want?" he panted.

"Just a word with the boss, don't stress yourself Joe, it's not good for the arteries."

The office door opened behind him. Stiletto heels struck the floor.

"Well look what the cat dragged in," a voice called from behind.

"Riva, my darling, I think you get more beautiful each time I see you," Roxy charmed.

"James Roxton, as smooth talking as usual. What can we do for you?"

Roxy pursed his lips. "How's about one of your specials?"

Her smirk grew and she gestured that he follow her to the bar, swaying her hips as she walked. She was a damn fine looking woman and Roxy had almost forgotten what he came in for. She handed him a drink and watched eagerly as he tried it.

"Absolutely divine, and the drink isn't that bad either."

"You here to see Pinky then?"

"I'll settle for a seat here staring at you all day if he's not around."

She sighed. "You know I'm old enough to be your mother, don't you? How is she? I heard what happened."

"Oh you know mum, she'll bounce back. She'd be out of hospital by now except she mentioned something about a young doctor's backside that has caught her fancy."

Riva laughed. "Lulu's a hard woman to keep down. Give her my best won't you." She gestured to the back door. "Go on, he's waiting for you."

Pinky was at his desk when Roxy walked in. He toyed with a cup of coffee, real coffee, not the stuff they tried to sell in the rest of the city. He didn't offer Roxy a cup.

In the general scheme of things Roxy would have been more than happy to see Pinky Morris up to his knees in concrete and indulging in a bit of deep sea diving. He was pretty sure Pinky thought the same about him. But they were both mutual club owners, both men of a certain way of life and traditions. Even with thirty years between them they were more alike than most of the people in S'aven. And out of a truce eventually comes respect.

"Roxy, take a seat."

"You know why I'm here?"

"Yes, I heard about what happened at Lulu's," Pinky said with an air of indifference. "How is your mother?"

"Recovering."

"I should send her some flowers."

"She'd appreciate chocolates more." As Roxy took a seat, he couldn't help but wonder whether he was sitting in John or Charlie's place.

"So, I hear your man Donnie Boom is back in town."

"Who told you that?"

Roxy checked his dirty nails. "Two of our girls spotted a man matching his description. Hideously scarred, red haired Scotsman with an enthusiasm for explosives. Not that I am ever one to cast aspersions, but you can probably follow my train of thought."

"Donnie dropped off the map seven years ago."

"I know. Right after he killed your brother. But I'm guessing, if you didn't take him out of the picture, there's a good chance he's back." Roxy sat back, trying to work out what was going through Pinky's head. The guy was so difficult to read.

"And you think that Donnie is back and is the one who blew up Lulu's?"

"Unless you know another insane Scot missing an eye and half their fingers." Roxy leaned forward. He wasn't a gangster, he wasn't even considered a dangerous man in S'aven, but Roxy had popularity and friends in the right places. He knew how the city worked and he knew the line he was walking was hairline at best. But Donnie Boom had put his mother in the hospital and there were some things men just couldn't be allowed to walk away from.

"The thing is Pinky, I'm a suspicious man. Not outright paranoid I'll grant you, but when a man comes back from the dead just to take out my mum my first thought is *why?*" Roxy paused. Pinky wasn't giving anything away.

"I'm curious, what did you come up with?"

He shrugged. "I know about the troubles Mum had with Frank and I know she wasn't entirely innocent in the conflict between you back then. I've got to ask you Pinky, face to face, because I respect you. Did you take a hit out on her?"

"I have no problem with your mother Roxy. She's a good business woman. I have no reason to want her dead." Pinky's hand flattened a beige file on his desk nonchalantly.

Roxy sighed in relief. For a minute there he felt like he'd been walking along the edge of a full scale war. He started to laugh. "I'm sure glad to hear you say that, Pinky. We're happy with the way things are in S'aven, it would be a damn shame if things should come to blows for something that has been seven years forgotten."

"Not forgotten," Pinky corrected. "Forgiven."

"You understand I've got to take Donnie out. He's got to pay. I'd really appreciate it if I could have your blessing."

Pinky put his cup down. He leaned back in his chair – the master in the room.

"Now you see Roxy, this is where we hit a bit of a problem. If Donnie is, as you say, back, then it's got to be me who is going to deal with him."

"Do you know where he is?"

Pinky didn't answer.

"Then I guess it's first come first serve."

"If my men need dealing with I'll deal with them."

"So you'll take care of *your* man?"

"If something needs to be taken care of I will do it."

It wasn't the answer Roxy was looking for. He regarded the other man suspiciously. There was more going on than Roxy knew. On the wall there were pictures of the good old days, when Pinky and his brother were terrorising S'aven like they owned the place.

"Mum and Frank." Roxy patted his legs. "That is some jaded history there. First she worked for him. He knocked her about. She stole his girls, set up on her own. Happened to do a lot better." Roxy started to laugh to himself. "Do you remember when he sent his guys to smash up her place?"

Pinky wasn't amused. "As I recall it was the week before he died." There was a threatening tone to his voice, but it wasn't in Roxy's nature to back down.

"Seem to remember that your brother was blown apart by one Donald Mac-crazy-Boom."

"That's what the people say," Pinky replied.

"Which makes me curious, given he's back in town with both his kneecaps functioning. Not to mention taking out old Morris grudges."

"Curiosity is a dangerous thing Roxy."

"What can I say, I'm an adrenaline seeker. The way I see it, Pinky, is I'm doing you a favour. Donnie Boom took out your brother, I end him and the situation is dealt with. You send Mum chocolates, she'll send you a fruit basket and we'll all go carolling at Christmas."

Again Pinky's hand touched the beige file. He was hiding something – protecting something.

"How old are you Roxy? Twenty-eight, twenty-nine?"

"Thirty-one," Roxy corrected.

"You're a youngster and I respect your mother enough not to kick you back into the gutter you crawled out of. I've seen you on the streets, you're a loner and eventually you'll end up riding the current to a watery grave. Guys like you burn out quickly, so quickly men like me don't need to give you a second thought." Pinky rested forward on his desk. "You get involved in this situation and you will disappear Roxy, only unlike Donnie you won't be coming back."

Roxy started to laugh at the absurdity of the threat. "I guess there's nothing more to say then. I'm sorry we couldn't come to an understanding." He offered to shake the other man's hand.

Then Pinky struck. For an old guy he moved fast. Roxy didn't even see it coming. His hand was pinned against the desktop. All of Pinky's strength holding it in place; the gangster's wiry fingers pinching through the fleshy dips in Roxy's wrist. He knew how to make it hurt. Roxy was about to retaliate and that's when he saw the cleaver. Somehow the old man had got hold of it, or maybe it had been there all along. Either way it was hovering over Roxy's fingers.

"Do you think I got here by taking shit off whoresons like you? You are just the product of my business. Your slag of a mother got stuck with you because she was on her back for me, you fucking pathetic bastard!"

He rested the blade on Roxy's knuckles. It was heavy and sharp.

"I heard a rumour you were musical Roxy, a bit of a piano player when the mood struck you. Do you think you'll miss it?" He raised the cleaver.

Roxy squeezed his eyes shut. Pinky smacked him in the face with the back of the handle. He fell back on the floor, dragging most of the desk with him. His head was swimming but his hand was free and attached. He looked up at Pinky. The frail old man in the yellow cardigan glared at him with wild eyes.

"You're going to leave S'aven for a while James. Take your mother away, come back after the winter. Or it won't be just pieces of you they find scattered across the city; there'll be pieces of her too."

Roxy clambered up off the floor. He was covered in papers. He brushed them off as he stood up and then stopped. On the floor there was a picture of a girl in scrubs leaving St Mary's Hospital. There was writing underneath the photograph and the hand was all too familiar.

He glanced at Pinky and wiped the blood dripping from the corner of his mouth. There were times for cocky comments, but when the psychopath blocking the doorway was holding a large cleaver it was better to just play scared.

"Okay, okay. I'm sorry. I'll leave tonight."

Roxy could scurry like a refugee fleeing from a water cannon when he had to. He made a show of it for the men in the club. Let them think he was afraid and out of his depth. Let them think he wasn't a threat. Let them be surprised. The outside world hit him and the coward fell away.

He swaggered up the road, humming to himself, the picture of the girl hung in his head. There was something familiar about her; he just couldn't put his finger on what it was. He lit up another cigarette and drew several drags hoping it would jog his memory. The girl remained a mystery, but the handwriting at least was a no-brainer. The Smith brothers were working for Pinky Morris. They would know who the girl was. Roxy licked his lips. And if Pinky Morris wanted the mystery girl Roxy would get to her first. This was the end of their truce. This was war.

* * *

Pinky gathered up the file as his wife joined him. She stood in the doorway with her arms folded. The meat cleaver hadn't escaped her attention and it was clear she didn't approve.

"What did he want?" She asked.

"Donnie Boom."

"Understandable given what Donnie did. We don't need Roxy causing us trouble."

"I shook the kid up, he's out of the picture," Pinky replied nonchalantly. He was pleased with himself. It had been a long time since someone had looked at him like he was a genuine threat.

"I still think you should cut Donnie loose, we don't need him."

"Not until we have the girl. And that won't be long. The Smith Brothers think they've found her." He fished out Rachel's photograph and handed it to her.

"She's got her sister's eyes," Riva said regretfully. "Do they know about her powers?"

"No, that's between us alone."

"Us and Donnie," Riva replied.

"Not for too much longer."

Pinky took the picture back. Things would be different, he promised himself. He knew where his brother went wrong and he wouldn't make those same mistakes. Roxy was scared of him, and soon the rest of the city would be too.

10

Rachel arrived in S'aven a month after her seventeenth birthday. As she shuffled off the train at Trinity Station her head had been an onslaught of naïve ambitions and excitement. The convent was gone and she was free. Soon she would be with her sister and the world would be theirs. But it never happened. Her sister was killed, and instead of liberation S'aven became just another prison; bigger, noisier and more dangerous.

As Rachel waited in that same station, seven years later, watching the rats duel with the pigeons, she realised it would be the same wherever she went. The prison was countrywide because she was a prisoner on the run and that would never change. They blamed Reachers for everything; she was guilty by nature and no jury would ever say otherwise.

Police marched up and down the boardwalk, shining lights on those huddled around their worn suitcases or battered sacks. They checked the faces of the men and women, even the children, looking for fugitives. People only left S'aven when they had to. It was the cops' job to work out what they were running from.

She could see them questioning a couple, checking their bags over and over while the husband insisted they were just going to see family. His wife was pretty, and the cops were enjoying making her squirm. They made the couple turn, press their hands against the wall. They only bothered to search the wife, laughing as her husband protested their innocence. She was smart though; she told him to be quiet–a quick feel was better than getting shot in the head.

"Do you want to know why we're leaving? Because of this!" The husband yelled.

With other cops this would have been a step too far, but these two were in good humour. They released the woman, squeezing her backside as she gathered her things. Then they wished them luck – a couple like that were going to need it.

Then it was time to move on. Their flashlights darted about as they headed towards the end of the platform. They passed two men in suits. There was no talk, the men held out a roll of notes, the cops took it and moved on. Rachel sat away from them all, she rested her head back and closed her eyes as they started to approach. They never even looked her way.

The train was running late. There were rumours about insurgents commandeering the northern lines and taking passengers hostage. The longer the delays, the more people remembered what was outside the city walls. S'aven had civilisation and work and food. It was right beside London where people still had money and the world still ran like it was supposed to. But outside the border, beyond the protection of the rational south there was so much unknown. Rachel stared at the arched exit out of the city; for her at least, it was the lesser of two evils.

She turned her head to the station entrance and that's when she saw him hobbling around the platform. He balanced on the crutch and scanned the crowd just like the cops had done. His bloodshot eyes looked panicked, maybe even desperate. She knew he was looking for her, she just wasn't sure why.

Then he spotted her, seeing through her powers, seeing just her, alone. The connection was instantaneous, it was like staring at a long lost twin. And it had been so long since she had felt anything more than emptiness.

He made his way over. He looked tired, but relieved to see her.

"Mind if I join you?"

"Why not," she replied and shifted so he could sit down. "It was David, wasn't it?"

"Yeah, but you can call me Charlie," he told her.

"I see. So that's your real name."

"Well it's the name most people know me by," he said with a shrug.

Rachel stared at the empty exit. "So what are you doing here, Charlie? Making sure I get out safe and sound?"

Charlie rubbed the back of his neck. In the distance they could hear the rumbling train hurtling their way. The platform shuffled into life.

"Actually I came to stop you."

Rachel scowled. "To stop me?"

"There's a rule amongst Reachers. It's kind of unwritten and I think I might be the only one who still abides by it, but we look after our own kind."

"Well, you have done your duty, you warned me to get out of the city so here I go. Bye-bye."

He took a deep breath which made her nervous. In the hospital he had been confident and insistent, the lack of certainty he was showing her now did little to put her at ease.

"It's not going to be safe for you outside of the city either," he confessed.

The train rolled into the station with an air of impatience. A muffled voice echoed through the speakers, but it was too distorted for Rachel to make out. She grabbed her bag and turned to Charlie.

"You have thirty seconds to tell me what the hell is going on or I get on that train and leave this shit-hole behind me."

"What do you know about Pinky Morris?"

She stared at him blankly. "Absolutely nothing. Pinky what?"

Charlie paused, surprised. "You don't know him at all?"

"Do you think I'd forget a name like Pinky Morris? Who is he?"

"He's an unpleasant gangster, one you don't want to get on the wrong side of. He hired me to find you."

Her scowl deepened.

"I didn't know what you were until it was too late. When I realised in the hospital I panicked. I figured if you left the city you could escape, but he has your picture and your name. It won't take long for him to find you again."

There was genuine fear in his eyes. He was scared for her, even more than she was for herself. The passengers around her were making their temporary escape. The survivalist in her wanted to join them, but this man was a Reacher and she hadn't been with her own kind for so long.

"So what would you have me do?"

"I know someone who can help you. There are safe places you can hide. I can help you get there."

"And why would you help me?"

"It's the least I can do, considering. And because we're the same."

The last call for the train bounded across the station. Apart from the police they were alone on the platform. Her father had warned her that times would come when she'd have no time to think. She closed her eyes and felt the neglected power within her.

"Kiss me," she finally said.

"Excuse me."

She rolled her eyes. "Don't get yourself excited, old man. Before you knew we had something in common you were ready to sell me out to an *unpleasant gangster I don't want to get on the wrong side of.* You've given me two fake names and you're an addict. I may be desperate but I am not stupid. Now kiss me and keep your thoughts open or I am getting on that train and your conscience can mourn my passing."

His mouth dropped open. She leaned forward anyway, sealing her lips around his. The physical intimacy shattered immediately as his memories flooded her mind. He was intent on saving her; she got that in the instant their mouths met. Not just saving her, he wanted to put things right. It meant so much to him, more than it should, but that was because of something else. She saw a woman, her face flickering from life to death. Her clothes changed as her belly swelled and then she blossomed in circles of blood. At her side was her miniature, a little girl with blond ringlets and rosy cheeks. Only waves of shadow kept stealing her. Rachel felt a pang in her heart as Charlie's loss struck her. She could take more of his mind and unravel him as a man, but this was more than she ever wanted to see. She pulled away and stared into his sad eyes.

The connection between them was strengthening. Reachers were drawn together, that's what made them so easy to hunt. The pull towards Charlie was already overpowering her common sense.

"Okay, if I go with you I'm going to lay down a few ground rules," she said, keen to establish some control.

His smirk started to overcome the general awkwardness of the kiss. "Rules?"

"You don't lie to me about anything, and if I decide to walk you won't stop me." She held out her hand, challenging Charlie to oppose her.

"Is that it?"

"No, I get to add to the rules when I see fit."

"Okay, deal." He took her hand.

As they shook on it she felt something shift within her, as though deciding to stay in S'aven had rearranged her thoughts and instincts. The need to flee was subsiding, but she was still uneasy sitting on that platform. She was in danger, serious danger, and she was putting her trust in a man with more issues than *the Voice* daily newspaper.

He was broken and tormented, not to mention an addict. Even though she had seen that he wanted to help her, she still couldn't totally trust him to make the right decision. He wanted to save her because he couldn't save his wife and child–what would happen if he failed her too? She sucked on her lower lip, thinking about what she had seen when they kissed. For now he was all she had and she was too much of a pragmatist to ignore him. "What happens now?"

"We figure out what the hell is going on and try to stay alive."

She let out an amused laugh–he made it sound so simple. "Good. Excellent plan. You lead the way."

11

Jackie Walters and Mickey Walters, no relation, sat in a white pickup at the entrance to Tower 8. There was rope in the back of the car and both men were armed. This was a new job for Mickey and he was nervous. The gun reminded him of his time in the service, before the disciplinary. He didn't want to mess up his first job, he was young and needed the money, but he also needed something to take his mind off what happened out in the Middle East; what he saw, what he did. Taking his cue off his partner for the night he tried to relax with a few nips of vodka to steady his nerves. Slowly it was working.

Jackie was an old hand. He'd been doing Pinky Morris' dirty work for so long his hands were black. In the good old days, when Frank Morris was running the show and Jackie's knees were still good, he was considered as dangerous as his boss, but those times were long over. He was well past his prime and, if he was honest, he was waiting for the Morris' to cut him loose.

"Car?" Mickey guessed.

"Nope." Jackie shifted in his seat. He had needed a piss for nearly an hour and his bladder was about to betray him.

"Clouds?"

"No."

"Hey Jackie, who's Donnie Boom?"

"Why you asking?"

"I heard a couple of the lads saying they heard he was back in town. They weren't too happy about it."

"Well, they wouldn't be. Donnie Boom set the bomb that killed Frank Morris."

"Pinky's brother?"

Jackie didn't dignify that with an answer.

"So are we going to take this Boom guy out then?"

"Jesus Christ, who do you think you are, Mafioso? We're not taking anyone out."

Mickey gulped. "Did you know him?"

"Yeah I knew him mad son of a bitch. Worked with him too, though I'd prefer working with a pack of rabid dogs. Still, the guy, crazy as he was, was as loyal to Frank Morris as any lapdog."

"So why did he kill him?"

"The question is why, after setting the bomb, did Donnie Boom run back into the building and blow half his head off? And that is a question the likes of you and me don't try and answer if we know what is good for us."

Mickey sighed. He glanced up at the tower. There were a number of lights flickering into life; families settling in for another night in their cramped homes. He watched the nearest window as a man went to his fridge. Mickey clicked his fingers excitedly.

"Kitchen?"

"Kitchen begins with a 'K' you dumb bastard. I need to water the flowers, stay here and keep your eyes peeled."

"What if she comes back?"

"Just watch her. Don't move from this spot until I get back." Jackie opened the door. It was getting colder in the city. The bite to the air painfully struck his cheeks as he wandered away from the towers, towards the small canal running alongside the apartment blocks. A pedestrian bridge crossed the river, illuminated by a weak solar lamp. It gave just enough light for him to find his way and not fall on his ass in a puddle of shitty water.

* * *

Charlie knew her file inside out. The seven years of her life in S'aven were mapped out on crisp white pages, clearly labelled in John's precise handwriting. But those pages did nothing to prepare Charlie for her smart mouthed, no-nonsense back-chat. She wasn't scared of him, whether that was because of the kiss, or the crutch–he couldn't decide. But it was clear, from the moment they walked out of the station, she was not going to sit in the back and do what she was told.

He liked her. Without a doubt she'd cause him no end of headaches, but he was already taken with her. She had a sense of humour which he hadn't expected from someone who had spent most of her life in hiding. She was smart too—a lot smarter than Charlie had been at her age. In the right hands she could go places. But as soon as he started to think those thoughts he scolded himself. People didn't last long in his line of work, and the last thing he needed was another death on his conscience.

Trinity Station was a half hour walk from Rachel's apartment. He was hoping John was there already. He was hoping by the time he got there he'd have some idea what they were going to do next.

"So what is it that you actually do? Are you like a private detective?" Rachel asked as they headed towards the canal separating the towers from the industrial wasteland. The darkness hid the swirling, putrid water, but nothing could stop the rotten smell stretching out across the causeway.

"I source things that are difficult to get."

"Not just people then?"

"Very rarely people. Mostly it's information or secrets."

"And they hire you because of your powers?"

"Sometimes. Mostly they know about my reputation. They know I deliver and that they can trust me. A lot of the work is just knowing where to look. I rarely have to use my powers at all. Which is lucky for me."

They reached the footbridge arching over the canal.

"Why's that?" Rachel stepped up the bridge. She turned to offer Charlie a hand.

"You've seen me; I'm not exactly in my prime anymore."

"The injury affects your powers?"

Charlie heaved himself up, taking her hand for just a second. "I'm just not what I was," he said hoping she would take the hint.

She did. "So do you know why this Mr Pink wants me?"

"Pinky Morris," Charlie corrected. "No, I don't. He didn't tell me when I was hired, and I didn't ask." Which he knew was his biggest mistake. Instead of trying to impress Pinky he should have given himself more time to research the job properly. Once again hindsight was gloating.

* * *

Jackie had lost himself in the moment, then he heard talking coming over the bridge above him. Snapping to attention he put his dick away, zipped up his fly and was about to head back to the van. Then he heard a name. It took his mind less than a second to work out who was coming over. Pinky had told him about the brothers he'd hired. He'd mentioned that Jackie should watch out for them, just in case. He was an old hand, an experienced hand, his knees were shot, but his senses were on the money. This was why Pinky had entrusted him with collecting the girl.

They were getting closer. He held the gun tighter. The girl's feet touched the top step. He began to count. One. Two. He rose.

* * *

The man came from nowhere. His shadow was wide and short. In his hand he held a snub pistol and pointed it at Charlie. It was a steady, uncompromising hand.

"Easy mate," Charlie said. "Wallet's in my pocket, we don't want any trouble, you can help yourself."

"Rachel Aaron?" The gunman said.

Charlie felt his stomach lurch. With his free hand he clutched the railings of the bridge and slowly tried to edge himself closer to Rachel.

"You've got the wrong girl," Charlie started, although he knew it was futile. He'd given Pinky his best pictures of her, there was no way they wouldn't recognise her.

"Shut up. You're both coming with me. Keep your hands where I can see them or I'll shoot you."

Rachel stepped forward before Charlie could stop her. "You won't shoot me," she said.

"Rachel, don't," Charlie warned.

"You won't shoot me."

She reached out calmly. It was like being back in the hospital, only this wasn't a confused, frightened addict she was up against. Before she could touch him his arm was wrapped around her shoulders. He was a big guy and he knew how to keep her pinned. The barrel of the gun pressed into the side of her face before Charlie could stumble down the bridge steps.

"You're not going to shoot her, Pinky wants her alive."

Realising he was right, the gun moved towards Charlie instead. "The boss doesn't have any sentiments towards you, though."

Suddenly something sliced through the air. The arms around Rachel wavered and she fell forward, dropping to her knees. Charlie reached for the gun and crawled towards her. He looked up and the darkness around them materialised into a shadow he would recognise anywhere. He stuffed the gun into his belt and helped Rachel to her feet.

"Jesus fucking Christ, John!" Charlie exclaimed. "Sometimes I think you're not happy on a job unless someone ends up dead!"

John nudged the body with his foot. "Sorry, I didn't realise you wanted him to shoot you. I'll remember next time." He shrugged and bent down to inspect the man's pockets.

"It's you!" Rachel gasped at John, she started backing away.

It was then that Charlie remembered they had met before. He reached out for her. "It's okay, it's okay. This is John, my brother. He's on our side."

"Your brother?"

"We need to move the bodies. There'll be another patrol heading this way in forty minutes."

Charlie noticed the plural. He hoped Rachel hadn't. He retrieved his crutch and helped John as best he could to heave the body up. They carried the corpse quickly through the foliage towards the towers. Rachel staggered behind.

"Let's get him in the van."

Before the doors were opened Charlie knew what would be in the back. The second man had a single shot to his skull, engorged by John fishing the bullet out. They slumped the older man inside. When Charlie closed the van door Rachel was behind him. She'd seen everything.

Charlie forced a nervous smile, trying to find something to say to make John seem less of a psychopath.

"They were here for me," she murmured, her face paled and she looked at Charlie with fear in her eyes.

"We need to get you inside before someone sees." Charlie turned to John. "We're going to need an alibi to cover our asses. I'm going to head over to the Cage, make sure people see me."

John nodded his head in agreement. "Pinky did invite you."

"Free drinks, I'd be a fool not to take him up on it."

"Do I get to ditch the bodies then?"

"No, stay with Rachel. Take her home. I'll be back."

"Hey, wait!" Rachel shouted. "He's just killed two men and you're leaving me with him!"

"In fairness, he's also saved your life twice. I'd say it's a level playing field. But if Pinky Morris finds out we've taken out his men this whole thing is going to go south and we will all be screwed. Nothing will happen to you if you stay with John, I promise." He gripped her shoulder in reassurance. "Now, get going before someone sees you together."

With a twitch of his head John gestured for her to move. She did so reluctantly, and if Charlie was honest he couldn't blame her hesitation. His brother did give off an air of a ruthless sociopath sometimes.

12

The taste of Charlie was still on her lips.

It was a bittersweet taste, which made her heart jump a little. As she hurried up the stairs to her apartment she ran her tongue over the memory. He was in so much pain. The agony was more than any painkillers could help with and deep down he knew this. But beneath the guilt and self-loathing Charlie was, at heart, a good man, he had to be–otherwise he wouldn't blame himself for everything that happened. And he would look after her; with his dying breath he would see her safe. She could trust him, and he was the first man she had come across since her father who had that quality.

The man behind her though–he was impossible to read. He followed her up the stairs, matching her pace so they were never sharing the same step. It was only when they reached her floor that she actually got a chance to look at him. He was taller than Charlie and his hair and complexion were darker. Although Charlie had all the charisma, John had all the looks in the family. He was lean, but muscular, with purpose and precision in his every movement. But offsetting his breathtakingly good looks were dark, cold eyes. As Rachel gawped at him she couldn't tell what he was thinking and it frightened her.

They reached her front door and she fumbled again for the keys, remembering last night and how he had made her struggle to open the door then too. Finally she got it open and paused.

"My boyfriend…"

"He left for his shift with his partner twenty-five minutes ago," John stated without disguising the impatience in his voice. His calculating eyes flickered across the corridor.

Rachel let him inside before he forced his way through.

"Wait by the door," he instructed. He reached into his coat and pulled out his gun. Rachel gasped, feeling ridiculous for doing so. It was by no way the first time she had seen one, but it was probably the first time she had seen anyone look so comfortable holding one.

"Put the door on the latch," John called after he'd finished his inspection.

She did as she was asked. When she turned around he was at the window, watching the street below.

"What is it?"

"Nothing. The street is empty." He checked his watch. "But Pinky could send more men."

"What happens then?"

He turned to her and frowned. "You should shower and change. You have blood on you."

Her hands wiped her cheeks and came away red. Quickly she hurried into the bathroom. The right side of her face was speckled red, joined by two finger streaks of blood across her forehead. Desperate to separate herself from what had happened she pulled her clothes free and kicked them into the corner. She ran the shower, receiving an initial tepid surge and then an icy trickle. In the shower her body began to shudder. She was going into shock.

"Come on, Rachel," she told herself. "Get a grip. You know what this is. Get a grip." The water ran red and then clear. She switched it off and wrapped herself in a towel. The collar of her jumper was smeared with blood but the rest of her clothes had at least survived the murder. She redressed herself quickly and threw the jumper into the wash basket.

There was no noise coming from the other room. She pressed herself against the door, wondering if he'd left and debating whether that would be good news or not. He'd saved her life, twice as Charlie had pointed out. But he had killed two men and there wasn't the slightest hint of remorse in him. Charlie was suffocating with guilt, but his brother seemed incapable of the emotion. Did that make him a bad man?

Rachel closed her eyes as a sinking feeling struck her. It didn't matter if John was bad or not, he was the only protection she had. She had to be pragmatic if she was going to make it out of S'aven alive. She forced a deep breath into her lungs. She would not be intimidated.

John was still standing by the window. He didn't move as she entered the room, nor as she finished getting dressed, although when she'd finished she realised he'd found Mark's bottle of vodka and poured her some in a tin cup. He held it out to her, still concentrating on the street below.

"Thanks." She necked the drink and handed him back the cup, hoping maybe he'd pour her another one–she sure as hell needed it. He didn't. "Still nothing?" She asked.

"Still nothing." John's body was tense though, as if he was expecting trouble at any minute.

"That's good, isn't it?" Rachel said, trying to diffuse the tension.

"It's better to be moving, instead of sitting here waiting to be caught," he grumbled and checked the window again impatiently. If Rachel didn't know better she'd suspect he wanted something to happen.

"You sound like my dad," she murmured and poured herself another shot of vodka.

He glanced at her curiously.

"Anyway, I'm Rachel Aaron." She held out her hand, but John ignored it.

"I know. I've been following you for a fortnight."

She tried not to let the comment unnerve her. They were in her home, and she was sick and tired of being scared. "I know. And you are?"

John turned back to the window. "Charlie told you."

"John, right?"

He nodded curtly.

"John, what?"

"Smith."

She sighed. "Of course, John Smith, I should have guessed. I'm getting the impression that you're not happy about helping me."

John turned back to the window. "I'm not happy about this job. We shouldn't have taken it."

"Then why did you?"

"We need the money."

"How much are you being paid?"

"Should have been thirty thousand," John grumbled.

"Jesus, someone was willing to pay that much to find me? They should have just put an ad out in the paper, I'd have come of my own volition."

"We don't know what they want with you," John said, turning back to her.

"For thirty grand I don't think I'd care."

"Yeah well, Charlie cares."

She sensed that maybe a tiny bit of him cared too.

"Okay, here's what I'll do then. I will pay you thirty grand in instalments to make up for it over ... let's say the next sixty years."

He raised his brow, she hoped in amusement. The coldness in his eyes started to evaporate. Rachel felt her cheeks blush when she realised she was staring.

"Wow, thirty grand. What were you going to spend it on?" She said.

John paused, as though he were considering whether or not it was wise to tell her. Eventually, he turned away. She expected the silence to remain, but it didn't.

"We need money to find Charlie's daughter."

Rachel sobered. "She's alive?"

"That's what we're trying to find out."

"What about his wife?"

John's jaw seemed to tighten. "She's dead. We don't know what happened to Lilly, but she was a Reacher so it doesn't take a genius to work it out. They send you all to the labs to be made safe."

The grief was consuming him as much as it was his brother. He was trying to hide it from her, from Charlie too, probably even from himself, but constant pain was difficult to mask. She reached out to comfort him and stopped. Her hand hovered over his. She dared herself to touch him. The contact was like a volt of electricity. She jumped back, her fingertips tingling. She'd never felt anything like it before.

"You're not a Reacher like Charlie."

He shook his head.

"But you're something else. What are you?"

The frosty eyes were back. "You ask a lot of questions."

"Well you have an entire file on me, I'm just playing catch up. Listen, I'm sorry you've lost the money. I wouldn't blame you if you wanted to turn me in. In fact, I'm beginning to think maybe to save a little girl it might be worth it."

"It's going to take a lot more than thirty grand to buy what we need. This was about getting Charlie back. He needs to be on form if we..." He stopped, distracted by the movement outside. "Oh, that's just fucking great. Get your coat, we're moving out."

* * *

Two officers took the first sweep of the towers. Beams of flashlights lit up the usual crannies. This was their beat. They knew where the kids hung out, where the tramps tried to stay warm. They knew the people they could move on, the ones they could get money out of and the ones to leave well alone.

As they passed the spattering of decrepit vehicles, a newcomer drew their attention. The white beacon shone like a warning light to their paranoia. It shouldn't be there. For a few minutes they dallied at a distance, daring each other to get closer until, eventually, the weakest of the pair gingerly inspected the tinted windscreen. A sealed off van was bad news. The other officer radioed it in.

There were too many bombs exploding over the city to suspect anything else. In minutes a diffusion team would arrive. The officers turned their attention to the surrounding towers, drawn to the possibility of a lure bomb.

* * *

Blue and red flashes flickered against the kitchen curtains. Rachel didn't have time to think about them, John was already walking out the door. He didn't seem to be rushing, but she had to hurry to catch him in the corridor.

"Hey, where are we going?"

"Away from here."

"Why?"

"They think there's a bomb in the van." John pushed open the door to the stairwell and listened.

"But there isn't."

Instantly he was on her, pushing her into the wall and allowing the stairwell door to isolate them again.

"The police are going to start searching the towers. We cannot be here." He stared at her intensely. "If you want to make it out alive you need do everything I say."

Rachel swallowed the lump in her throat. He wasn't hurting her, but she could feel the strength in his body. She leaned forward and pressed her lips against his. He pulled away immediately, but it was enough to know she could count on him. She smiled sheepishly under his confused frown.

"Okay, I trust you," she whispered. "Lead the way."

"Don't make a sound," he said with a deep scowl etched into his face. He gave her a strange look and resumed his place by the door.

He waited in the doorway. Rachel held her breath. There were noises from the surrounding apartments. Small bursts of life filtered through the thin walls, oblivious to the drama unfolding outside. Something drew John's attention. He nodded to Rachel. She slipped into the stairwell as he eased the door closed. She was about to move down the stairs when he stopped her.

Silently John sped up two floors. It didn't make any sense, they were going to get trapped. She hurried after him, catching up only when he stopped dead. He was listening again. Something was happening below them. He pressed his finger to his lips and gestured that they continue.

Another flight conquered, but the sounds were creeping up after them. It sounded like more police had arrived. John seemed to think so too. He reached the fourth floor above Rachel's and side stepped into the next corridor. His movements were so precise it was like he'd done this before. Rachel clumsily followed. She hit the door too hard, banging it against the wall.

John flinched. He gave her a warning look, one that made her never want to get on his bad side. Carefully, she closed the door behind her. This corridor was different. A fire exit sulked in the corner. Rachel stared at it, wondering what the people on this floor had done to get the additional health and safety benefits.

As John pushed open the door the icy air knocked the breath out of her. She realised then that she was sweating. John reached out his hand impatiently.

The fire exit led to a small, precariously secured metal ladder. Rachel looked at it and broke a smile.

"You're joking, right?"

"It's safe," he said as he pulled out a pair of leather gloves. He passed them to her. "Put these on and climb down after me. Go careful but quick."

The ground taunted her sixteen stories below. The drop would see her body splattered across the cracked pavement. She wouldn't even feel it. As she climbed out onto the building's side her head started to spin. She realised not being able to feel her death was no comfort. Her gloved fingers struggled to grasp the ladder. She felt herself slipping and her stomach lurched. It was enough to propel her forwards. She clutched onto the metal and sucked in the air through her chattering teeth. The exit was out of her reach. The only way was down.

Even with the gloves the ladder was freezing. Rachel's hands were stinging by the third rung. John clasped the side of the ladder as he descended. If the cold bothered him he wasn't showing it. He held on with his bare hands, moving down at a steady rhythm. At least six feet beneath her already, he would reach the ground before she even made it half way.

Rachel's arms were already burning. The air whipped at her, tearing her hair from its plait. She was shivering as the sweat froze against her skin. The ladder creaked with her every movement. She'd lost count of the floors. The ground was nearer. If she fell now it would be a slow death. She'd feel the breaks in her bones when she hit the ground. Maybe she'd stay conscious, aware of her life as it spilled out over the concrete. She swallowed and continued moving.

"Rachel, stop," John hissed.

She glanced down. Two cops were sweeping the pavement below her. Their flashlights danced around the surrounding bushes. John was pressing himself against the wall. Rachel did the same. She closed her eyes. Held her breath. And waited.

The footsteps of the officers echoed through the wind. She heard them talking. They were nervous. It should have been a routine patrol, an easy night for the pair of them. *Damn terrorists*. Their footsteps faded. Rachel dared to peek. Red and blue flashes grew fiercer around the corner. If John was right they would already be securing the area. Mostly the police were useless, but the recent bombings had changed things.

"Okay, move," John whispered. "Quickly, we're running out of time."

With a breath to steady what was left of her nerves, she dropped down another rung. Her hands were shaking in the panic. John would reach the bottom and he would have to wait for her. With the police circling the building he couldn't afford to do that. She had to move faster or she'd get them both caught.

Fighting against the aches in her body, she matched John's pace. He was nearly at the bottom and she was about to join him. Then her foot struck the next rung too hard. She slipped. Her legs kicked out into nothingness. She was going to fall. Her mouth opened to scream, but a hand closed around it. Her body was pressed into the wall; secured back on the treacherous ladder.

John had a tight hold on her. His body overlapped hers. She had no idea how he had reached her so quickly, and at that moment she didn't care. His breathing was steady, his heart rate calm. It was infectious. Rachel felt herself relax against him. They were still alive. It probably wouldn't last, but for the second she could enjoy it.

"Ready?" he said, releasing her.

"Yeah, let's do this."

The final rungs were in sight. If she jumped she would probably just sprain an ankle. John jumped clear, landing like a cat on the ground. He reached out to help her join him. Her feet touched solid earth and she stopped herself from dropping to her knees and kissing the ground.

"I can't believe I did that," she said.

"Let's move."

He led the way around the back of the building, keeping close to the wall. When they reached the corner he leaned over and instantly fell back.

"What is it?"

"They're coming back." His head frantically turned to find an escape. But there wasn't one.

He grabbed her hand, meaning to drag her back the way they had come. It was useless. They were trapped. She pulled John back, pushing him against the wall this time. He was about to fight her and then they heard their footsteps.

"You have to relax and trust me this time," she whispered. "Close your eyes. You're not here."

John was at least a foot and a half taller than her. She stood in front of him regardless. Her arms slotted under his, tucking him in to a tight hug. She closed her eyes and the harsh concrete block dissolved. She was six years old, sitting in the snow, clutching her older sister for dear life. Men in balaclavas walked through the wood around them. *Not here, not here, not here,* she had said.

The officers turned the corner. The nerves through her back started to tingle. If they were doing their jobs properly they might see her and John, and it wouldn't matter how hard she tried. But if they were lax, if they thought they had already cleared the building, their guard would be down.

"Not here, not here, not here," she murmured until there were no other words in the world.

"It'll be kids," one cop said to the other. "Bet you anything, goddamn stupid kids."

Their boots crunched against the gravel. Two steps away. One step. Rachel held her breath. Her grip around John tightened. *Not here, not here.* The footsteps stopped. Rachel felt John's heart rate increase. She squeezed him harder. He couldn't buckle, she wouldn't let him.

"Fancy a smoke before the big guns arrive?" One of the cops said.

She listened as he rummaged through his uniform. A match was struck. She smelt smoke. They were standing right there, less than an arm length away and they still hadn't noticed anything amiss. She felt John's body loosen. The officers smoked and grunted at each other. Their idle chit-chat was as impressive as their observational skills. Rachel opened one eye impatiently. *Back to work, back to work, back to work.*

Like puppets they stamped out their cigarettes. Their trudging steps struck the pavement. In seconds they were gone. John subtly coughed. She realised she was still clutching him tightly. Reluctantly she released him and shivered at the loss of warmth. John's mouth twitched in a rare smirk.

"You can make yourself invisible?"

"Yes, well no, not invisible, more unnoticeable." She wiped the sweat from her forehead with her sleeve. "Learned that after months of running away from insurgents."

John looked surprised, and Rachel couldn't help but feel smug. They thought they knew everything about her; they had barely scratched the surface.

"Why were you running away from insurgents?" John said, gesturing that they should keep walking, heading back towards the canal.

"We took a wrong turn. I don't really remember the hows and whys. My parents had a farm in Red Forest." She didn't have to elaborate. Most people had heard about the fighting in Red Forest, how the insurgents tried to move in and how the military tried to stop them. How anyone in the middle ended up in a mass grave. Few really understood exactly what happened.

"How old were you?"

"About six. I just remember my father being so determined we had to get to S'aven. He was worried about the military getting us. A guerrilla warrior shot him. That wasn't in your file was it?" She asked him, already knowing the answer.

The wind wasn't so bad at ground level but she was starting to shiver in the cold. As the remnants of red and blue disappeared under an urban horizon her adrenaline started to ebb. She realised how hungry she was and her body started to revolt against her.

"Are you okay?" John asked as she stumbled.

"I'm good," she said through chattering teeth.

John wrapped his coat around her without a word. She was starting to like him.

13

The queue outside the club curled around the next street. Roxy stood on the opposite side of the road, taking shelter outside the Chinese takeaway, blowing thick circles of smoke into the air. He'd been standing there for an hour, slowly building up an empathy with the hordes of scantily clad girls and boys shivering to get into the Cage. Patience had never been his strong point and he was regretting not factoring that into his plan for the night. Getting Donnie Boom was becoming an obsession. The more the Scotsman managed to elude him the more intent Roxy was to see the bastard dead.

His plan had initially been so simple he'd barely given it any thought. It seemed obvious that Pinky Morris would be grateful to have his brother's killer taken out. Roxy had even fantasized about a reward for his trouble. But that hadn't been the case. For some reason Donnie was protected and Roxy felt a growing desperation to find out why. It was that desperation that saw him standing in the freezing wind, watching for one of Pinky's boys to make an appearance at the club. He needed information and eventually, if he plied them with enough drinks, someone would start to talk.

But once again things weren't going his way. So far the only people jumping the rope were z-list celebrities and the usual socialite-waste-of-spaces who seemed to think the city couldn't exist without them. He hadn't seen a single face he could tie back to Pinky.

Roxy tossed his cigarette into the gutter. There was no point hanging about in the cold. If the boys were coming he'd meet them inside, to hell with Pinky seeing him. As he approached the door he smiled at the bouncers and their fat, pink faces. They were the runts of the Morris empire, expendable nobodies who had been left behind in the evening's exodus. If Pinky had ever told them anything important their thick skulls wouldn't remember. Both men knew Roxy on sight and their wide enthusiastic smiles were enough to convince Roxy they were totally ignorant of their boss's troubles.

"Evening, gentlemen," he said pushing the obligatory pound notes into their pockets. "Who's in the cage tonight?"

"Ivon the Terrible, fighting some army dropout, Cole something–doesn't really matter what his name is, he won't last long. You coming in?"

"Aye, better put a bit of money on Ivon or he'll think I don't like him."

That night the club was heaving. The fight in the cage was mirrored across the surrounding dance floor. Bookies bellowed their odds, punch after punch. Money slipped across tables while girls danced overhead. The music was lost in the chaos, only the vibration of the bass reached Roxy, rattling his body like an external heartbeat.

Ivon was a giant in the cage. The seven foot Nordic fighter slammed his bare fists into a bloody pulp that had once been his opponent. The game would end when the loser called time, forfeiting his fee and his reputation. Some men would rather die, some men did. As Roxy passed the cage his fingers twitched at the sight of the betting. If the night went downhill he'd have to make his own fun.

He made his way to the bar, winking and smiling at familiar or pretty faces. It may have been Pinky's club but it was Roxy's domain. He ordered himself a scotch and soda, giving the barman a tip to ensure he'd get a good drink and not a watered down glass of piss. From his new vantage point he spotted Pinky's wife disappearing out the back, her tight dress clinging to every curve of her body. He licked his lips at the thought of her.

His eyes drifted back to the fight, cruising over the spectators. Pinky's men usually held a table at the front of the cage, packed with girls young enough to be their granddaughters and enough coke to recreate the Alps. But today the table was occupied by a group of excitable Koreans, waving pound notes at the fighters as though they were flags. There wasn't a significant face in the building.

Then he spotted something that changed his mood. He downed his drink and ordered another. In the corner of the club, away from the excitement, sat his old friend Charlie Smith. Roxy felt a surge of emotion take him. That cocky asshole who had stolen his girlfriend. Charlie Smith–the man with a plan, the guy always in charge. Mr Know-it-all. Mr Can-do-no-wrong. Mr Arrives-home-to-find-wife-being-butchered-on-the-kitchen-table. They went back years. Good years, bad years, together they had been as thick as thieves. But the last time they had seen each other Charlie had been stabbed, his wife had been murdered, and Roxy felt about ready to finish him off. Those sentiments hadn't changed all that much.

Roxy licked his lips and pushed away his animosity. Opportunities favoured the impulsive and in six long strides he had already started to turn his luck around.

"Charlie Smith, as I live and breathe!" He bellowed over the noise. "You don't write, you don't call, anyone would think…" He sat down at Charlie's table and stopped.

A year ago, when Roxy stormed away from the Smith Brothers, Charlie was in a bad way. Things hadn't changed. If anything they'd got worse. His eyes were ringed red and bloodshot. Beneath his stubble his complexion was sickly and grey. He was a husk of the man Roxy had known.

"Holy shit, what grave did you crawl out of?" Roxy said in alarm.

"Roxy," Charlie said, his eyes were wide and surprised. He reached out to shake his friend's hand weakly. "Jesus, I didn't expect to see you here. You look good man, really good."

"I'd say you too, but I'd be lying," Roxy said. "Where's the sharply dressed one?" Roxy looked about the club for the other brother, coming up empty.

"He refused to come. Not really his scene."

"Not really yours either, old man," Roxy teased. "Last time we were in a place like this I seem to remember you falling asleep at the bar."

Charlie shook his head defensively. "Hey, it was pretty late and we'd been on the run for like twenty hours."

"Semantics," Roxy said. "I didn't figure you would be coming back to S'aven, John made it pretty clear you guys were retiring."

Charlie shifted his beer from one hand to the other. "Best laid plans I guess. There's not much out there for men like us to do. How are you keeping anyway?"

"You know me," Roxy said, sipping his drink. "Always on the up."

"You working?"

"Here and there, nothing like the old days, but I get by."

"And your mum?"

"She's good," he lied. "On vacation for the winter."

They sat in an awkward silence. The air between them was still thick, no matter how much Roxy pretended it wasn't. It would need to be cleared, or he would at least need to clear it enough to ease Charlie's conscience. He was mulling over the best way to broach the last words he had shouted at Charlie:

"You better hope you don't make it, Charlie, because I will fucking kill you. You hear me? If I ever see you again you will wish you died here."

But he was too slow, Charlie broke the silence. "I suppose you're here to kill me."

Roxy laughed; before things went bad he and Charlie had been good friends. "Maybe if I was a man of my word, but you know what I'm like, Charlie. Listen, what I said back then, well I..."

"You meant every word, Roxy. And you have every right to say what you did. I would have said the same. You loved Sarah as much as I did, I don't blame you for hating me."

"Yeah, but she wouldn't have wanted me to be such a drama queen about it. I'm not saying it wasn't your fault, but you didn't mean for it to happen. Back then I was still in shock, she was my ex-girlfriend, my best friend and she was suddenly gone." Roxy let out an involuntary shudder.

"It should have been me."

Roxy couldn't bring himself to lie. "Yes, it should. If it had to happen to one of you, it should have been you," he agreed. "But even you didn't deserve to go like that. Jesus, I'm not sure I know anyone who does." He swallowed the bitterness rising in the back of his throat. He never saw Sarah's body, just the look on John's face when he described what they did to her. For the briefest moment he felt a pang of guilt. Strapped to a chair, as battered as his wife, Charlie had been forced to watch as they peeled back the skin from her trembling bones. Nobody deserved that.

"You left before I could thank you," Charlie said. "I know that you were angry with me. I know that what happened was my fault, but you still helped John get me out of hospital. You didn't have to do that."

Roxy sighed. "No, I did. They would have come back for you as soon as they found out you were alive."

"All the more reason to stay out of it."

"It's not every day the great John Smith comes asking for help. He had to swallow a lot of pride that night," he said, smiling to himself. "I just kept looking at your brother's big brown puppy dog eyes and thinking if you died too I'd be stuck looking after him."

Charlie started to laugh. "Still I appreciate it. I owe you."

"It's what friends do, or so I'm told. I'm glad you're alright, Charlie. I really am. What about my little Lilly-Pad? Still no news on what happened to her?"

Charlie's eyes saddened. "We've got a contact who might be able to help. But they want a lot of cash for the information."

"They know you're looking for a six year old girl right?"

"They know and they don't care. They heard what we had pulled off in the past and they assume that we can just shit out wads of money on demand."

Roxy paused. "You know there was a time when you could. I remember the days when the infamous Smith Brothers could do just about anything, with the help from their incredible associates, of course," he said with a wink.

Charlie patted his lame leg. "Not anymore. This is our first job since, well, you know. We spent the last year hunting for Lilly and the first lead we get demands a quarter of a million upfront. I've been out of the game so long even if I didn't have the body of an eighty year old war veteran I'd still be useless."

"Nothing a bit of a shave wouldn't fix," Roxy teased. "Besides you weren't exactly Ivon the Terrible back in the day."

Charlie frowned. "Who's Ivon the Terrible?"

"Doesn't matter. You guys always worked in the same way. John was the muscle, you were the brains and, of course, occasionally I was the creative genius that made everything all the more fun." Even Roxy couldn't deny that the old team had been a good one. He still missed the camaraderie and excitement of the old days.

"And Sarah kept us all together," Charlie said sadly. "Without her we all fell apart and the work dried up."

"But you're working a job now, right?"

"Oh yeah, we took a run of the mill find-and-locate job that has blown up righteously in our faces. Now we're not going to get paid. Hell, we're going to be lucky if we make it out of S'aven in one piece."

Roxy gave Charlie his most empathetic look. "Come on, Charlie I know you and you're just deliberately falling at the first hurdle. Look, who're you working for?" He made it sound like he was just asking out of courtesy, trying to help an old friend.

Charlie paused and then shrugged, he'd always trusted Roxy more than he should. "Pinky Morris."

Roxy feigned surprise. "Well, it's no wonder you're not getting paid. You'll have more luck getting John into flip-flops than getting Pinky to pay out. But Pinky's a dinosaur, clinging on to a life that doesn't exist in this town anymore. He's probably just playing difficult to make himself feel like a big man. You and John could take him down in your sleep. And you know it too. Listen if things get out of hand give me a call. I know Pinky fairly well, I could put in a word for you if you don't want to get your hands dirty, but I promise you, Charlie, you can take him."

"That's a turnaround from wanting me dead," Charlie remarked.

"My friend, your imminent death is on hold until you find Lilly. If I can help get her back then I will. You just have to ask, you know. I've got your back, right, always have, otherwise your brother would kill me. You want another drink?"

Before Charlie could answer his phone vibrated in his pocket. Charlie checked the caller ID and frowned.

He answered. "John. What's up?" His frown deepened. "You're where? Jesus, what the hell happened? So you left ... Yeah, I know there were cops ... Okay, okay ... No I suppose you couldn't ... Just stay where you are ... I don't know, I'll think of something. Is Rachel okay? Good, look after her. I'll be with you soon." He hung up the phone and put his head in his hands.

"Let me guess, things taken a turn for the worst?"

"You could say that. There were cops at our mark's address. John panicked."

"Ah, I see. Were they after him?"

"Not knowingly, but you know how he is. One flash of red and blue and he disappears in a cloud of smoke."

"Cop phobic. I'm sure there's a name for that." Roxy chuckled. "Still I suppose, given he's like the world's most wanted man, he probably is entitled to freak out."

Charlie shrugged and then nodded in agreement. "And now he's roaming the streets with nowhere to go."

Roxy nodded sympathetically. "Well I've got a couch. John wouldn't touch it with a barge pole but you're welcome to crash at my place, and he can just stand in the corner with his usual disapproving look on his face."

Charlie sighed, as though he were contemplating whether he should take up the offer or not. Roxy gave his best "caring, nonchalant face."

Eventually he shook his head. "Probably not a good idea. There's a girl with us and she needs to lie low. John's trawling the industrial district with her at this minute."

"Pretty boy like John, he could solve your money worries in a night there."

Charlie stood up. "I've got to go."

"Hold your horses, pet. I've got this covered. Now, I don't usually drive this sober but for you I'll make an exception. I've got a lockup down there you can hole up in. You can fill me in on the details on the way."

"Roxy I can't ask you to do that. This girl, she's in trouble. Big trouble. You don't want to get yourself involved."

Roxy dismissed the warning. "Listen to me, Charlie Smith, what kind of friend would I be if I didn't at least offer to help? Besides, I love trouble–we get on like a house on fire."

Charlie hesitated briefly. "I'm not even sure what the cut on the job is going to be."

"I'll do it for the look on John's face alone."

Roxy let Charlie take the lead. Charlie liked to think he was in charge and he would until it was too late. As they reached the door Roxy couldn't help himself. He turned back to the club and caught Riva's eye as she returned to the bar. It could all blow up in his face, so it was important to enjoy himself when he had the opportunity.

14

Seven years ago Pablo had walked into Pinky's den. He had looked Pinky in the eye and told him Frank Morris was dead. There were cops outside waiting to break the news, but Pablo had insisted the news came from him. The cops, the rest of his boys, even Riva never saw Pinky react, they never saw the despair or the relief in his eyes.

And through everything, as business started to dive, as the Russians took over, as Pinky lost his throne, Pablo stayed by his side, watching his boss's back like an obedient dog.

Pinky stared at him now, taking in his ridiculous hat and pointed shoes and felt that he never really knew Pablo. He couldn't understand why a man would follow with such loyalty and expect to go nowhere. But as they stood together now, standing in Pinky's new warehouse, it was starting to become clearer.

The closer Pablo got the more he learned. Pinky had shared everything with him, every business deal, every paranoia, and Pablo had been his counsel, Pablo had steered him; controlled him. And now he was trying to do it again.

Pablo had drawn Pinky aside, taken him into the back office while the others waited outside. This new venture was supposed to impress them, showing them that things were going to change, but Pablo was going to put an end to that–well he could try.

"Jackie told me he was picking up a girl for you," Pablo said, the accusation rich in his tone.

"Jackie's got a big mouth." Not for much longer, Pinky thought to himself.

"Yeah well it's not Jackie we need to worry about. I know Donnie Boom is back and I know he put you onto this girl."

Pinky folded his arms. "You seem to be poking your nose where it's not wanted."

Pablo sighed. He took off his hat, clasping it to his chest. "Pinky, you got me worried. You've been taking bad deals; some of the boys say they haven't had their cut. I know things are tough, but we always had things under control before."

"I had things under control," Pinky snapped. "I have things under control. Tomorrow everything is going to change."

Pablo licked his lips nervously. "She's a Reacher, isn't she?"

He glared at Pablo as though he had just blasphemed. Nobody was supposed to know about the girl.

"Pinky, don't do this. When Frank brought that Reacher in it nearly destroyed you. It nearly destroyed us all. She came in, she got into our heads, turned us against each other. You must remember what it was like with her breathing down our necks all the time, trying to find out all of our secrets. The men out there aren't going to stand for it, not with business the way it is."

Pinky understood now. This wasn't about the girl at all. Pablo had something to hide, something he didn't want Pinky to find out about. Pinky shook his head; he had allowed this man to get too close. It was a problem he needed to solve.

"Reachers made us what we were," Pinky said to himself more than anything.

"No Pinky, Reachers ruined you, and I'm not hanging around to watch history repeat itself. If you bring that girl here, if she starts getting inside our heads, I'm out, Pinky."

Pinky turned away and examined the rest of his men as they talked in the main body of the warehouse. They all had secrets. He met Fat Joe's eye, his cousin and his bookkeeper. He trusted the man with his money, but then he'd trusted Pablo. He checked his watch. In a few hours he would have the girl and he wouldn't have to rely on trust anymore. He would know for certain that they were loyal.

He wouldn't be like Frank, though, he would keep the girl a secret. The men would never know what she really was. He glanced back at Pablo. He would ensure they never knew.

"Then we're done," Pinky finally said.

Pablo sighed, shook his head and reached for the door. "I'm sorry it has to be this way, Pinky." He left, walking out of the warehouse without a word to the others.

Pinky leaned in the doorway, the men looked confused. They respected Pablo, he was the reason a lot of them rode out the hard times.

"Lee," Pinky called.

Lee Hart was the youngest there, but what he lacked in experience he made up for in enthusiasm. He followed Pinky into the office.

"Close the door."

Lee did what he was told. He always did what he was told, and maybe sometimes he didn't do it as well as Pinky would have liked, but he was still obedient. He would never stand in the way of Pinky and his ambition.

"What's up, boss?"

"What's your plan, Lee?"

Lee frowned. "Boss?"

"Yeah. When I was your age I had it all planned out. Me and my brother were going to own the city." Pinky smiled. "We did it too. We owned S'aven. I have one regret—I never had a son." He paused, waiting for Lee to take the bait.

"Things are changing, Lee. The time has come to take back the city again. But I'm an old man; once I've reclaimed my city I will need someone to pass it on to."

Lee finally understood. His eyes sparkled with ambition.

"I need good men around me, Lee. Men I can trust."

"I've got your back, boss. Whatever you need."

Pinky forced a smile. "That's good to hear. Especially today. Do you know what happened to my brother?"

"Frank, yeah. I heard that Donnie Boom put a bomb under his table when he was at dinner." Lee shifted awkwardly.

"And you've heard Donnie is back."

Lee nodded, his mouth opening and closing like a suffocating fish. He couldn't look Pinky in the eye and shifted from one foot to the other awkwardly.

Pinky beckoned him closer, putting his hand around Lee's shoulders. He hadn't been lying about wanting a son. It would have been nice to have a protégée, having someone to carry on the family name. He looked Lee in the eye—if he did find someone it wasn't going to be him.

"What if I was to tell you Donnie didn't kill my brother. What would you say if I told you Pablo killed Frank?"

The colour drained from Lee's face, his mouth dangled open like a dead fish's. "Pablo?" He squeaked.

"The thing about being boss is you have to deal with these problems, it doesn't matter how you feel about it. Do you think you could deal with a problem like this?"

Lee thought about it, and then nodded arrogantly. "Sure boss, I could deal with it."

"How would you deal with it?"

There was only one way to deal with it, even Lee couldn't miss that. "Take him out."

Pinky nodded approvingly and waited for Lee's statement to sink in.

"You want me to take him out?"

"That depends, Lee, what's your plan? Do you want to fill my shoes one day, or are you happy just sitting in the bottom of the heap?"

The decision was made. Lee stood a little taller, knowing that the next few hours could be the making of him.

"Consider it done, boss."

* * *

He'd killed a man before. There was a fight, Lee had thrown the first punch and the guy went down, cracking his skull on the pavement. He was dead instantly. Lee didn't even mean to do it. But he did, and that made him a killer.

The others thought he was stupid, but Pinky had seen the real him. And even better Pinky had given him the chance to show the others what Lee Hart could actually do. He had his gun; he was standing outside Pablo's apartment. He could do this.

His hand was trembling as it knocked. He waited, tapping his foot as the seconds passed. Pablo opened the door. He frowned at Lee and then sighed.

"You'd better come in," he said and stepped aside for Lee.

They walked into his sitting room. Pablo sat in his favourite chair. He was drinking. He didn't offer Lee anything.

"I should have left when Frank started to lose it," Pablo suddenly said. "I don't know if that Reacher messed with his head, or if he was just crazy anyway. I should have just left. But I didn't. I stayed. I slogged it out. Helped Pinky when the whole business started falling apart. Jesus, you boys would be coming to me, expecting to get paid, and I'd talk my way out of it, knowing there wasn't any money." Pablo laughed and shook his head.

Lee watched him. It looked as if he'd been crying. He couldn't imagine Pablo crying. His stomach lurched; what if Pablo started begging for his life? He swallowed his nerves and reached for his gun.

"It's all going to happen again. Whatever happened to Frank is happening to Pinky. If you were smart you'd get out while you still can."

But Lee wasn't smart. He aimed the barrel of the gun at Pablo's head. He could barely keep it steady.

"I'm sorry," he murmured and pulled the trigger.

* * *

Pinky inspected the latest shipment of heroin with the remnants of his men. They were laughing and making jokes, but seemed nervous around Pinky. Let them be, Pinky thought to himself, if they had something to hide he would soon find out about it. His phone started to ring. He was expecting it to be Jackie, maybe Lee, but it was Riva.

"Pinky, we've got a problem. Charlie Smith just left the club with Roxy."

It should have surprised him, but it didn't. The men around him went silent, waiting for the fallout.

"When?"

"A few minutes ago."

"No word from Jackie?"

"Nothing yet. I tried calling him but there was no answer. Maybe we should send Pablo."

Pinky cleared his throat. "Pablo's no longer with us."

His men stopped what they were doing. The air in the warehouse chilled.

"What do you mean not with us?" Riva paused. "Pinky, no."

He hung up his phone. All he needed was the girl. Nothing else mattered.

15

John insisted they wait out in the cold and Rachel was too tired to argue. They sat on a heap of bricks, the remains of an old garage, surrounded by miles of containers and lockups. The place was a storage maze, big enough to hide in. They'd lost the cops quickly and so far nobody else had tracked them down. Rachel was beginning to think they might survive the night, until the wind blew in from the sea. She tightened John's coat around herself and tried to subtly huddle closer to him.

"This place is nice," she said drawing her legs up away from the discarded needles and condoms on the tarmac.

"The factory owners pay for hired protection so the cops don't bother coming this way."

"What about gangsters?"

"They won't look for us here. This place is reserved for people who no longer give a fuck. We won't be bothered."

They wouldn't be bothered because John was terrifying. He was her protection and even she was scared of him. She shivered against the bricks, but he didn't move. His eyes fixed on the road ahead.

"Aren't you cold?" She whispered.

"No."

"What, are you a robot or something?"

"Or something," his mouth twitched, hinting at a smile and a little bit of her unease melted away. "I thought you'd be tougher, being from Red Forest."

"Screw you," she replied with a smirk. "I saved your ass back there. How tough do I have to be?"

"After I saved your ass you mean, what's it now, three times?"

"You're living in the past, John."

His smile broke free and suddenly he was human. Sure, he could shoot a man through the head with his eyes closed, but he had a sense of humour–what else really mattered? She nudged him with her foot and he playfully slapped it away, shooting her a scowl that would probably make most people soil themselves.

"Do you do it often? Use your powers?" John suddenly asked.

"Probably more often than I should," Rachel replied.

"You could do well in our line of work," he mused. "We could use you."

Rachel stared at him, trying to see if he was serious. She tightened the coat around herself. She was cold, hungry, and alive. It felt good, and she started to smile.

Eventually he looked at her thoughtfully. "You turned around to face me that night, why?"

"I was sick of you terrorising me," she replied and folded her arms defiantly. She had forgotten about that, although now she couldn't quite muster the energy to hold a grudge against him.

"You knew I was there?" He sounded hurt.

"Yeah, I could feel you. You'd follow me at the same place every time I left work."

He shook his head, angry at himself.

Rachel reached out and touched his arm. The sensation was different, warmer somehow. "Hey, it's probably just my heightened senses. I'm sure you are a very good stalker."

Headlights waved across the road ahead.

Rachel squeezed his arm tighter. "Here we go again."

The car pulled up with a skid. She used her powers, muttering her mantra over her chattering teeth.

"This time it doesn't count," John whispered. He nudged her and pointed at the men getting out of the car. "It's Charlie."

As she ungracefully leapt over the hepatitis concrete she realised that Charlie wasn't alone. Another man was getting out the driver's seat. John tensed and she stopped in her tracks. She touched John's arm, to feel his reaction, to know when she needed to duck.

"What's he doing here?" John's voice was venomous.

"Anyone would think he didn't miss me," the stranger called out.

Rachel tried to see the man through the headlights, but all she could make out was a broad shadow leaning against the bonnet of the car. John reached for his gun and instinctively she stepped behind him.

"John, put that away!" It was Charlie's orders. And it was clearly an order he was used to bellowing.

"I said I'd shoot him next time I saw him."

"Yes and he said he'd kill me. While I'm alive, he's alive. Look, you know if it wasn't for him I'd be dead already, so just relax. Okay?" Charlie stepped free of the beaming lights focusing on his brother. "John, okay?"

John conceded, albeit reluctantly. "What's he doing here?"

"Helping us out, God knows we need it. You good?"

John nodded.

"You sure?"

"Yes, I'm fucking sure." John shook his head; he glanced back at Rachel and rolled his eyes.

The gesture made Charlie frown. He was looking more tired and run down than ever. Rachel didn't have to guess why.

"You okay, Charlie?" She whispered.

He didn't try to hide it from her. "Same old. Did John take good care of you?"

She opened her arms wide. "Still in one piece, with minimal psychological damage."

"Good to hear. This is a good friend of ours." Charlie ignored John's scoff. "Roxy, say hello."

Everything about Roxy suggested Charlie had pulled him off a three-day drinking binge. His suit was filthy and stank of smoke. He hadn't shaved and his hair brush seemed to be on strike. He was good looking; in the way drug addled rock stars tend to be. But then charm can disguise anything and with Roxy it hid just about every fault he had.

"An absolute pleasure to meet you, sweetheart. Hop in before we let all the heat out."

"Where are we going?" John growled.

"Somewhere safe," Charlie reassured him. "Just get in the car and stop being an asshole."

There was a rule about cars and strangers. But it was cold and Rachel had decided about an hour ago she'd rather die in the warmth. The backseat was a graveyard for discarded coffee cups and pizza boxes. She kicked the rubbish to the floor. The others were still in a stalemate outside. The good, the bad, and the ugly; only she couldn't work out which was which.

"Hey guys, I appreciate you've got to flex your muscles at each other, but I'm freezing my ass off in here!" She shouted.

John was the first to get in. He slumped beside her and stared at the pile of rubbish at his feet. The dismay on his face was adorable. There was no way he could be the ugly.

"Don't worry, I've got your back," she whispered. She may not have felt the instant connection with John like she had with Charlie, but he had climbed down a building with her and she was still in his coat.

He looked appreciative, at least until the others got in.

"Roxy's got a place where we can lie low," Charlie said, taking the front passenger seat.

"It's nothing fancy, but I have heat, maybe even a bottle of bourbon if we're lucky." Roxy gave Rachel a wink.

"And what's it going to cost us?" John snapped as the car pulled away.

"Just the pleasure of your delightful company, my love."

Charlie turned to the backseat. "Stop sulking and play nice, Roxy didn't have to help us."

"I don't trust him," John growled.

"You don't like him. There's a difference."

"I don't like him because I don't trust him. And he's an asshole," John added.

* * *

Factories and warehouses dominated the edge of S'aven, blowing smoke into the smog as though they were working in cahoots. There was always work going on in the estate. Twelve hour shifts of intense physical labour for half the minimum wage and a free chunk of bread at break. The work was hard and it was dangerous. If you showed up late you lost your spot and you'd go hungry for the day, but at least you wouldn't get crushed, or burned, or maimed, or poisoned.

The whole place stank like rotten eggs and putrid meat, even away from the factories and towards the storage units, the air burned like acid on the nose. The electricity shorted more than it worked, and around the lockups the lights were always out. Most of the containers were locked up tight, but that didn't stop thieves from trying their luck. People who paid for storage obviously had something worth keeping and, if there was a gap in security, containers could be emptied in seconds.

They pulled up outside Roxy's garage and Charlie breathed an audible sigh. The trembling in his hands was getting out of control.

Roxy tossed a set of keys at John. "Be a dear and open her up."

Charlie knew his brother well enough to decipher the grumbling noises as he made his way out of the car. The garage door was open and Roxy rolled the car inside. The headlights lit up the dusty contents and Charlie flinched as they nearly hit a stuffed tiger sandwiched between two mannequins.

"Don't mind old Monty," Roxy laughed. "He's just there to scare off thieves. There's a generator on the left, should have enough gas to keep the lights on for a day or two," he shouted at John as he switched off the engine.

In seconds the room flickered into light. Charlie hobbled out of the car, stumbling on piles of boxes. He knocked one to the floor and a whole stack of forged identity passes scattered over the floor. Against the walls more random assortments of junk were piled up. Paintings and rolled up carpets rested alongside a crossbow, ready to launch a firework at two garden gnomes on the far side of the room. A wall of boxes, six foot deep protected them from stacks of old DVD's and even some VHS tapes, haphazardly stacked in jaunty towers.

"Jesus, Rox' what the hell have you got in here?" Charlie said, keeping his voice down in case the junk decided to avalanche.

"Mostly the boxes are just porn," Roxy shrugged, "Buyer fell through at the last minute, and now I can't shift them. They're yours for half my asking fee if you want them," he added. "Anyway you guys can hole up here for as long as you want," Roxy offered.

"Here?" John snapped.

"Hey, I know it's not a five star hotel or anything…"

"No, it's a trap is what it is."

Charlie pinched the bridge of his nose. They were always like this, bickering like children and competing for attention. His headache was growing; it was nearly time for his medication. Then he panicked. He couldn't take his pills with them all watching. One of them would notice. "It's not a trap, John," he said in frustration.

"So what, he just shows up and offers to help out of the kindness of his heart?"

"It's very easy to do," Roxy said. "For those of us who have a heart. You know you're the one who tried to kill me. I should be the one angry with you."

"He tried to kill you!" Rachel exclaimed.

"No." John replied indignantly. "If I had tried to kill you, you would be dead. It was a through and through shot, as I intended, you barely felt it."

"Barely felt it!" Roxy scoffed.

"Guys please!" Charlie begged. The garage light was starting to hurt his eyes. He shouldn't have had that beer, it was messing with his head and now he couldn't think straight. "Nobody is double-crossing anyone. Nobody is killing anyone. Now sit down and shut up!" He glanced at Rachel like an exasperated parent.

Both men fell silent and took swipes at each other with their body language instead.

Roxy jumped onto the bonnet of his car. "So what's the game plan?" He asked Charlie directly.

The plan was to take his medication and then work out how to get out of the city alive. He wondered what they would say if he told them that. Roxy would call him out, John would walk away and Rachel, well she would probably stay with him until Pinky's boys caught up with them. Charlie had to rest against the boxes for support. The air was growing thick around him. He was hot—too hot.

"We're not telling you anything!" John barked when the silence started to drag.

"Oh, for crying out loud. If you don't want my help I'm not keeping you here. Go on, feel free to find your own hole to crawl into, one big enough to fit your giant ego in."

In desperation Charlie raised his hands. "Enough! Please. We've got to get Rachel to a church I know about in the morning. There's a convent she can go to where Pinky would never find her. Then we're getting the hell out of S'aven."

"What about the money?" Roxy asked.

"There you go, the real reason he's helping us!" John added.

"What money?" Charlie said.

"You said Pinky had offered you thirty grand for her, how are you going to get it?"

"I'm not."

Roxy started to laugh. "You're bullshitting me."

"Leave it," John growled.

"Leave it? You two need to raise a quarter of a million and you're turning away from an easy thirty grand. What the hell is wrong with you? Jesus, there was a time when you boys would take the girl, the money, and the kitchen sink."

"Yeah well times change," Charlie looked down at his leg in case Roxy still didn't get it.

"Did they have to remove your spine when you were in surgery?"

"That's it!" John was ready to strike.

Charlie pulled him aside. "Leave it."

"He doesn't get to say shit like that," John growled.

"But he's right. You know he's right." Charlie stared his brother in the eye. He was too scared to take the job. Too scared to realise that he was past it. Too scared to make the gamble with another life in his hands. He stared at John, feeling like a coward and a fraud. His brother had stuck by him through everything for nothing.

John shook his head. "He's not."

"I am right. You guys may be suffering some kind of brother amnesia but I remember how you guys worked, how we all worked together. You never backed down from a difficult job, you never took the easy way out, and there is no way Charlie would save the life of a girl he barely knows over his own daughter," Roxy said.

Rachel couldn't believe it. The thought of Charlie sacrificing his own daughter made her heart sink. She glared at Charlie, feeling like it was her own flesh and blood he was putting on the line. Charlie wanted to explain himself, but it was too late.

"Get the fuck out!" John yelled at Roxy before he could stir up more trouble.

"This is my fucking garage, you get out!"

"Shut up!" Rachel screamed. Her voice hit them in waves, slapping each one into silence. "You're all acting like goddamn children!"

Each man stared at her as though they had never seen her before. The plain girl who had shifted so easily into the background was now in charge.

"I am not going to a convent," she told them. "So factor that into your plan."

"The convent is safe…" Charlie started

"I spent half my life in a convent, Charlie. I know exactly what it is."

"Not all orgies and ritual sacrifice then?" Roxy chirped.

"Do you think I'd be so set against going if it was?" Rachel sighed.

Charlie rubbed his face desperately. "Then I can't keep you safe."

"You don't have to," John suddenly said. "She saved me tonight, she can look after herself."

"So what, you want to go after the money. Put Rachel's life on the line?" Charlie dared John to say he did.

"I want to go after the money," Rachel told him sternly. "I'm prepared to put my own life on the line."

"Yeah, well, I'm not," Charlie said.

"Charlie…" Rachel started.

"No. I'm not having your blood on my hands as well."

"Come on Charlie, she's not going to get hurt," Roxy shouted.

"You don't know that! We didn't think Sarah would get hurt, but she did."

"Sarah got hurt because you…"

John moved. He was so quick. Before Charlie knew what was happening his brother was between them both, staring Roxy down. This time Roxy backed off. He shook his head at them both.

"You know what, John, I'm not going to say anything. You know it already. You know exactly why Sarah died. And if Charlie is out of the game then what the hell are you still doing here? You don't need him," he said.

For months Charlie had been waiting to hear those words from someone. Roxy was right. John didn't need him, none of them did.

He was by the door before he realised he was leaving.

"Charlie, wait," Rachel called.

"I need to clear my head," he replied. And he left.

* * *

She had a suspicion Roxy had caused it all. Even if he hadn't, he was loving every minute of the drama. Charlie had been gone a while and it didn't look like he was coming back. Rachel guessed where he would be. The outburst and the lack of control had nothing to do with what was said and everything to do with the withdrawal he was starting to feel. She felt guilty for not going after him and foolish for thinking she could make any difference.

Beside her John's eyes were fixed on the garage door. His confidence had taken a beating. He may have been a deadly killing machine, but Roxy was wrong, he did need his brother. She put her hand on his, trying to ignore the urge to delve into his thoughts.

"If it makes it easier I can just go to the convent and bail after a couple of days."

He shook his head. "What you did tonight, could you do it again?"

"Yup, if you let me get my hands on Roxy I might even be able to just put him to sleep," she whispered.

John nearly laughed at that. "Charlie will be back when he's sorted his head out."

Roxy rifled around the boxes. He opened one, shook his head and pushed it towards Rachel. Then he reached for another. Rachel glanced inside. It was filled with blank identity passes. A pass like that would get her into London. She had no identification, nothing to prove she was even British. Neither of them was looking at her. She sat down idly beside the box and lifted one of the passes. She wasn't a natural thief, but she needed a backup plan.

"Ah, here we go," Roxy removed a bottle from one of the boxes. He twisted the bottle cap off and smelled it before he drank it. "You know it's not as bad as everyone says it is." He handed it to John and if looks could kill Roxy would have been flayed across the garage. "Rachel, drink?"

She took the bottle out of politeness and after stealing from the man she felt she owed him the courtesy. It tasted like fire. She gasped as it burned through her throat.

"God, that's awful," she gasped, but she took another mouthful, savouring the warmth in her chest. The liquid settled in her empty stomach and she started to swoon.

"Easy there, sweetheart, I know it has been a rough night, but there's no need to go crazy."

"This isn't a rough night," Rachel replied. "Eventful, tiring, maybe even fun, but not rough." She felt her eyelids starting to flag, it was always like this with her–she could push herself so far and then she'd just drop. "Definitely tiring."

"At least that is something I can do for you."

Roxy flung open the passenger seat door and ushered her inside. He made a pillow for her from a rolled up tapestry and used another to cover her tiny body. They smelt of smoke, which actually counteracted the general stench of the industrial estate. She settled into them as her body started to surrender.

"Get some rest, pet. Everything will be better in the morning."

He closed the door, cocooning her in a dull silence. She shifted on the back seat until her body relented. It was better than sleeping in a doorway somewhere. It was better than being at home. Her eyes buckled. She thought about Charlie and about saving a little girl. There was a future somewhere on that road, one she could live with.

16

Who was he to tell Rachel what she could and couldn't do? He wasn't her father. If she wanted to put her life at risk that was her business. Only it wasn't that straightforward. If anything happened to her, if she died at the hands of Pinky Morris, it would be too much. He had to protect her; it was built into his genes and probably built into hers. And if he thought he could do it, if he was certain he wouldn't end up putting her in danger, his head wouldn't be pounding quite so hard.

Charlie's legs started to buckle as he reached the edge of S'aven. He managed to haul himself to a bench overlooking a set of ramshackle sheds and collapsed. The pain in his head was so strong he couldn't even feel his back ache. He tried to get up and failed. What was the point in getting up, he had nowhere to go.

"Hey there," the voice was rich with insinuation.

Charlie turned his head. He could just about make out a girl with pink hair. She couldn't have been more than sixteen. She was wrapped in a thick coat, mittens, and a heavy scarf. When he looked again he realised she didn't have pink hair at all, she was just wearing a woollen hat. She sat down beside him without a hint of nervousness.

"Want something to take the edge off?"

It took him a minute to know what she was talking about. Then she withdrew a packet with two blue tablets inside and dangled it for him to paw at. He still had his medication. He didn't need to play a game of chance from some teenager who had the smarts to sell a product instead of her body. But he wanted to. Roulette meant it was out of his hands. Let God decide.

"What are they?"

"Something to make it all better. You got any money?"

He did have money. Not all of it, but enough. She took everything he had and he took everything she gave him.

Charlie opened his front door. He tried to remember how he'd managed to walk so far. There was music coming from the kitchen, a faint beat he recognised but couldn't put his finger on. He stepped into the hall, leaving his keys on the sideboard. Lilly had been scrawling at the walls again. She always drew dogs, four legs, a head and tail in as many colours as she could get her hands on. Charlie inspected the addition to the wallpaper with a smirk. The walls flickered red. Tiny, bloody handprints. He blinked and stared back at the dogs. He was getting a headache.

Sarah was chopping vegetables in the kitchen. She hummed along with the music, tone deaf and shameless of the fact. Charlie waited in the doorway, admiring the curve of her back and roundness of her buttocks. After Lilly was born she'd gained a bit of weight in the hips. It suited her.

"You're late," she said.

"I know, I'm sorry." Although that's not what he had originally said. The last time they'd had the conversation he'd been defensive and they'd argued.

Charlie stepped closer, willing his wife to turn around. "Smells good."

She sliced a carrot so fiercely it stopped him in his tracks. "Where were you?"

"Working, but I'm finished now. For good. No more jobs."

Slowly she placed the knife down. "No, you're not. And I would never make you, do you know why, Charlie? Because you would be miserable. You have to work. It's all you have."

"I have you and Lilly. Where is she?"

"Upstairs."

Charlie made to move.

"She's asleep."

"I'll just poke my head around the door."

"I've just gotten her down."

Charlie sighed. He just wanted to see his little girl again. It felt like he hadn't seen in her in so long.

"Okay," he said, relenting. "Do you want a hand?"

"You, cooking?"

"I never said I'd cook. I was thinking more like I could hold your hair while you chopped," Charlie said. He reached out, caressing her neck. She was hesitant against the first touch. Things were not good between them and they were only going to get worse, but he could snatch tender moments when they both just put their differences aside and remembered that they still loved each other. His lips found his way against her shoulder and she fell back into him.

"I've missed this," he whispered.

"Then why did you keep going back to *her*?" There was no anger in her voice. If anything, she pitied him.

"I don't know."

"I bet you didn't even suspect what she would do while you were fucking her!"

Charlie swallowed. Of course he never suspected. There's no way he'd have touched her if he had known she was going to murder his wife. He shouldn't have touched her at all.

"I'm sorry."

"You're always sorry," she snapped and pulled away from him.

Charlie looked down at his fingers. They were red with blood.

"Do you know how long they cut on me? Slice, slice, slice. They cut me for so long I didn't think there was anything left of me." She snatched up the knife again. "And they knew just how to do it, where it would hurt the most. Then they were going to do it to Lilly. 'Answer the question or we'll make her look like you.' And if I'd known the answer I would have sung it at the top of my voice."

"But they didn't kill Lilly," Charlie stated.

"No. They took her away to be experimented on like some goddamn animal. They just killed me. *She* killed me."

He knew it all already. He was there for most of it.

"I'm so sorry, Sarah. It should have been me."

"You're damn right it should."

Charlie turned away. It wasn't his wife. It wasn't her voice, or her words. He so wanted it to be, but he could never recreate her the way she was. His mind would never be that generous.

"And look at you now, moping about like you're the victim. Poor little Charlie Smith, carrying the weight of the world on his shoulders. No good to anyone. Not even his own daughter!"

"I'll get her back, Sarah. I promise you I will find her."

He could feel her behind him, pushing into his side as though she were really sitting with him. But she wasn't, and when he gathered up the courage to face her he remembered why. Her cheeks were slashed open, still dripping thick clots of blood onto the white shirt she had been wearing. The rest of her face was swollen purple, disguising the gap in her left socket where her eye should have been. Big brown eyes, he used to adore staring into them. Her untouched left hand scratched at the tacky blood on her right stump. The hand had been removed at the wrist. It went with one smooth slice. God, he had loved her and she had been so much more than this.

Sarah snorted. "You can't even take the first steps, Charlie. The Reacher girl was your best shot. But look at you, running away because you're too scared of *her* dying. Shame you didn't afford me that luxury."

"Rachel's so young," Charlie defended.

"No younger than I was when you dragged me into your life."

Charlie sighed. "You were different. I was different."

"It's no different. You saw me and you used me, Charlie."

"That's not true."

"Oh, really. So why did you leave me when I wanted out?"

He swallowed the rising bile in the back of his throat.

"Is it because she's a Reacher? Is that why she's too good to die for you?" Her voice was venomous. She reached out for him but Charlie moved away, backing towards the wall.

"You were too good to die like this. Because of me," he murmured, but those words would never matter to dead Sarah.

"You've finally found someone who might be able to help but you won't ask her, will you? You coward! You can screw your own family over, but not another Reacher!"

"It's not like that! I can't have another death on my conscience."

"Except your daughter's." Sarah folded her arms, the stump sticking out awkwardly towards him. "You're pathetic, Charlie. You always have been. I'd have stopped at nothing to get Lilly back home safe. And what are you going to do if you ever get her back? Let her join the family business?"

He slumped to the floor with his head in his hands.

"Look at you, someone stands up against you and you can't handle it. You have to run off and pop pills like some backstreet junkie."

"I'm not a junkie!"

"Baby, you are having a drug induced hallucination and this isn't even the first time it's happened. You know John knows about all this, he's just pretending everything's fine because he thinks you'll try and kill yourself, again."

"I didn't try and kill myself!" Charlie shouted.

"But John doesn't think that, does he? He saw you with that bottle of pills and he thought you were doing yourself in, doing what you should have done a year ago. What would he think, knowing that his big brother is a piece of shit addict?"

She leapt at him. The nails of her left hand scratched into his face. He pushed her back and she rolled across the floor, her broken legs clattering in the air. Her laugh was unholy.

"Why are you like this?"

"Because you made me this way." She sat up with unnatural ease. Her solitary brown eye glared at him with intensity.

"I don't know if I can save Lilly; she might be dead already."

"Oh boo hoo." Sarah poked out her bottom lip, " 'She might be dead already.' What kind of father would rest until he knew there was no hope?"

Charlie rubbed the scratches on his face. "Do you really think Rachel can help?"

Sarah rolled her eye and yawned. "How many times do I have to tell you; I am a figment of your imagination. I don't think anything."

"You're right," Charlie paused. "Or I'm right. She's what we need, someone with a clear head. And she wants to do it, from the minute she learned about Lilly, she wanted to help."

"If only you weren't about to overdose."

"What?"

"At least we'll be together again," she smiled, running her left hand over his face. Her image flickered again. If only he could remember what she was really like. If he could just hold onto what she had been.

He didn't want to die, not like this.

17

John didn't relax. Sitting on the boxes in the garage he seemed more wired than usual. Since he was a kid he'd relied on Charlie. Roxy had never understood it. John was stronger, smarter, faster. He didn't need Charlie, not like Charlie needed him, but without his big brother he was at a total loss. Roxy sometimes wondered what would have happened if Charlie hadn't made it through surgery a year ago. He tried to imagine what John would do, where he would go. It always seemed that one didn't exist without the other, but that wasn't the case. Charlie had his family and John had whatever it was he did when Charlie was being dad.

But now John was lost. There was a girl asleep in the back of the car who needed his help, but he wouldn't move without his brother. Roxy had seen this before, the night Charlie lay dying in an operating theatre and John couldn't even begin to formulate a plan of action to get his brother out of danger. With all his skill, as deadly as he was, he couldn't function without his brother telling him what to do. It made no sense, but nothing about John did.

"So why is Pinky after the girl?" Roxy said when the silence got too much.

"I don't know."

"What do you mean you don't know?"

"I mean I don't know. Do you want me to write it down in big letters for you?"

"What the hell are you thinking taking on a job without knowing the details? Who is she?"

John gave him a warning look.

"You don't know that either. Jesus Christ, what happened–you guys decided the leg work just isn't worth the effort? Come on, this is Charlie's speciality.

Guy used to know every card on the table before he even looked at his own hand. Hell, he really has lost it."

"Shut up."

"And you are in total denial, aren't you? John, your brother has screwed up and now you're in deep shit. And that girl is probably going to end up dead. Jesus, get angry for crying out loud. Do something instead of just sitting there."

"It's not his fault."

"No, of course not. It's never Charlie's fault. He's Mr Fucking-Perfect. Just like it wasn't his fault that Sarah died."

"It wasn't."

"Tell me how in the hell it wasn't his fault. He lets that harlot into his bed, and the next thing he knows she's cutting up Sarah in his kitchen. You tell me who I can blame for my best friend's death if I can't blame it on him?"

John looked up; his eyes were piercing. "You can blame it on me."

Roxy scoffed at the suggestion. It was just like John to carry all of his brother's burdens.

"They were looking for me," John suddenly confessed. "That was why the girl got to Charlie in the first place and then she cut up Sarah to get him to talk. They wanted to know where I was." John paused; every now and again his humanity would betray him. He glanced at Roxy, looking at his most vulnerable. "He never said a word. After everything they did to her. Would you have kept your mouth shut?"

Roxy was craving another cigarette. He'd always thought the bitch had just lost her head and started attacking her lover's wife for the fun of it. Charlie had met her; he'd had his affair, broken his marriage, and to put the icing on the cake, allowed his wife to get hacked into bits by his mistress. Now with John as the culprit Roxy couldn't quite muster up the same bitter hatred he'd been saving for Charlie.

"Why didn't you tell me?"

John shrugged. "Charlie didn't tell me. Not until he was better. We knew they'd catch up with us eventually, we just let our guard down."

"It's not your fault," he told John, meaning it.

"You were quick to blame Charlie, why not me?"

"Well, you're better looking. That helps. Seriously, I didn't realise. I don't know, maybe Charlie should have given you up, but it probably wouldn't have saved Sarah. And you think they took Lilly?"

"They're from the Institute; they were hardly going to leave her. We have to get her back, which has always been the plan. Charlie just needs to get back to form. Then we can think about going after her."

"All the more reason to run the job," Roxy murmured.

"Anyone connected with us is in danger. If Rachel comes in with us it's not just Pinky Morris that she will have to deal with. The Institute will stop at nothing to get to her because of me." John spared a glance at the car. "That goes for you as well."

"That girl is going to be on the run for the rest of her life. She's a Reacher, worse still, she's a Reacher with ambition. And although I appreciate your touching concern for my safety, I have no regard for my personal welfare so there is no reason for you to."

John scowled. "I don't."

"Good, 'cause I'd sell you out for half a pint. So what are you going to do now?"

"Wait for Charlie to come back."

Roxy laughed. "That's taking charge."

"Fuck you!"

"Hey, you're the one who's so dependent on your brother you can't even take a shit without his go ahead."

"It's called loyalty. Learn it and people might start covering your back again!"

"Here's a wakeup call, John, you're nothing without your half-crippled brother!"

There was a muffled shout from inside the car; Rachel telling them to shut up.

"You know I really like her. She's a lot feistier than she looks."

"Touch her and you're a dead man."

"Someone has a soft spot for her," Roxy teased. "You know I could find out who she is. Maybe even find out why she's so valuable to Mr Morris too."

"How?"

"You know me, pet, I have my ways. All you have to do is ask. Come morning I'll have all the answers and if you're very lucky, breakfast."

"Bullshit."

Roxy stood up and brushed the dirt from his clothes. "Prepare to eat your words, Johnny Boy."

"You're going now?"

"I'll give you and Miss Shout-At-Me-In-My-Own-Car a little alone time. Don't make a mess."

18

Donnie was in his lounge when Pinky made it home. Sitting in Pinky's armchair like he was a made man with nothing to worry about.

Pinky never understood why his brother kept the guy around. Donnie was wired on a different frequency to the rest of the world. He was a violent sociopath like the rest of the boys, but there was something else about him, something unsettling that Pinky had never been able to put his finger on.

Once he had Rachel he'd get rid of Donnie as quickly as he could. Let the girl inside Donnie's head for anything of worth and then blow it to pieces. Pinky smiled at his guest. Donnie was inspecting the only picture of Frank in the room. It was a photograph of Riva, sitting in the garden under a warm sun, but Frank and his girl just made it in the shot. Pinky couldn't remember ever sitting out in the back with his brother. He guessed it must have happened when he was away, clearing up his brother's mess while Frank played happy families in the sunshine.

"What brings you out here, Donnie?"

"You're picking her up tonight. I thought I'd be here," Donnie replied. His leg was twitching on the carpet, it was either out of excitement or nerve damage, Pinky couldn't tell.

"Is Riva here?"

Donnie shook his head. The next question: *how the hell did you get in here*, hung in the air. Pinky poured himself a drink. The doorbell rang. He checked his watch. It was probably Jackie coming to explain what the hell had gone wrong. Pinky didn't want to have to kill him as well.

"Get the door," Pinky said.

As he did, Pinky picked up the picture Donnie had been looking at. There were times when he hated Frank and his whore. Especially towards the end. It was funny, Frank's death had been a relief more than anything.

"It's a cop," Donnie announced, showing the officer inside.

Only it wasn't. It was a dirty cop. It was one of Pinky's dirty cops.

"Gary," Pinky said. It seemed this was the night for unwanted guests, Pinky topped up his drink–he was going to need it. "I take it you've got a reason for showing up here."

Gary, still in his uniform, shifted awkwardly. "Eh yeah, I'd thought you'd want to know straightaway. Jackie Walters and Mickey Walters are dead."

Somehow the news wasn't a surprise. Pinky took a seat, leaving the other two standing. His gaze drifted off to the far wall. A crack was starting to run through the paint. Riva had filled it countless times, but there it was again. The rest of the walls were papered, hiding the structural weakness of his home – his castle. He swirled his drink and stared at Gary.

"How?"

"Shot, both of them. Their van was parked outside block eight. Cops thought there was a bomb or something in it. When they opened it up they found the bodies inside."

"Any witnesses?"

"None."

"Did they have a girl with them?"

Gary shook his head. "Not that we found."

Pinky finished his drink. He held it out to Donnie for a refill.

"You came all this way to tell me this, Gary?"

"I thought you'd want to know."

"You don't have my number?"

Gary paused, suddenly not so self-assured. "Well the signal's down again and I thought, eh…"

"You didn't think," Donnie corrected. "Just showed up at the boss's house like you were somebody."

"Ignore him. I appreciate it, Gary." Pinky reached into his pocket and pulled out a wad of notes. He gave Gary a donation, one large enough to shut Donnie up. "You keep this news to yourself."

He didn't like Gary. A dirty cop was a snake, it didn't matter how many favours he did. And Gary was one of the really bad ones, a man you wouldn't trust with your daughter. The guy was a creep and a stupid one at that. If he wasn't winding Donnie up so much, Pinky would have kicked him out already.

"You want a drink, Gary?"

"Sure boss. That'd be great." Gary looked like he was about to get all his Christmas presents at once. He's probably been dreaming of this moment all his life, Pinky thought with a shake of his head.

"Fix him up, Donnie."

The look on Donnie's face was worth the hundred he'd given Gary.

"This is a great place," Gary said, settling himself into the room. His eyes wandered, admiring the lounge as though he knew everything about good taste. "Really nice."

Donnie shoved a drink at him angrily.

"Thanks. No, I mean it, Pinky. This place is awesome. My wife would kill for these carpets. Oh, wow, is this Riva?" Gary picked up the picture, looking at Pinky's wife like she was a lingerie model. Looking at her like her husband, a known killer, wasn't watching his every move.

Then his ogling shifted. He squinted at the scenery in confusion. "Rachel?" He asked himself aloud and shook his head when he took a closer look. Of course it wasn't Rachel. The picture was ten years old at least.

"What did you say?" Donnie hissed.

"Oh, just the girl in the picture. Looks just like my partner's piece." Gary chuckled to himself.

"What did you say her name was?" Pinky asked.

"Rachel."

"Rachel?"

"Aaron, I think. Yeah, Rachel Aaron." Gary smiled. "Right stuck up cow."

"Could she have killed Jackie Walters?" Pinky said.

"Rachel?" He laughed.

"What about her boyfriend? Your partner? Does he have a gun?"

"He might have, but I can't see Mark taking down anyone. Kid is soft as anything."

"Not even if two men were trying to haul his sweetheart away?"

Gary paused. "I don't know. Maybe. I guess he could have if he thought he had no choice."

Slowly questions where starting to form in Gary's head. Pinky could see the ideas morphing in the cop's slow, stinted expressions. He was putting pieces together; they just weren't making a picture yet.

"Sit down Gary, another drink?" Pinky poured another generous helping and watched as it filled Gary's cheeks with colour. "Have they started giving you cops guns yet?"

"No, only special forces. Cut backs." Gary leaned forward, ready to let his boss in on a big secret. "But we got a load off that shipment the Japanese got busted for."

"So you and your partner are armed?"

Gary nodded. "Yeah." He gave Pinky a worried look.

"Good to know you're protected," Pinky replied dismissively.

So Rachel's boyfriend had access to a weapon. But did he pull the trigger? Maybe she did it herself, she was a Reacher, and they were capable of everything. Then again it could have been the Smith Brothers, or Roxy. Too many names were getting tangled up in his business. Now Gary was embroiled in the unravelling disaster. It should have been a simple kidnap–bag over her head and all their problems were over. Now there were suspects, there were enemies, and he wouldn't be surprised if they were all out to get him and stop him taking back what was his. Well he'd show them, he'd get the girl and then they'd all be at his mercy.

Headlights beamed in through the open curtains, a two-minute warning that their business was coming to an end. Even Gary picked up the sign and downed his drink with gratitude. Pinky slipped him another hundred before he left. At least Gary could be paid off.

As he left Donnie shuffled forward. "Why didn't you ask him to bring in Rachel?"

"Him? I wouldn't ask him to clean my windows. The man's a fucking imbecile, he shows up at my home in his uniform!" Pinky shook his head. "I want you to follow him."

Donnie grunted.

"He doesn't know who she is. I want it to stay that way. Keep your eye on him; make sure he keeps his distance. Once we have her, we'll cut him loose."

"Sure thing, boss."

The front door opened. Riva was home. Pinky gave him the nod. Business was over.

* * *

Gary skipped out of Pinky's house. He counted the money greedily. With it he could pay his rent, maybe even get some fresh fruit in for the kids. But if he took it down to the betting shop he could double or maybe even triple it. In his head he was dividing up his winnings, he could buy a lot of girls, maybe even afford a night in Lulu's.

A hand grabbed his shoulder.

"Hold up. Boss has a job for you," Donnie told him.

Gary couldn't believe it. His day was just getting better and better. If he got two hundred for just passing on a message, how much would he get for doing an actual job? Maybe two nights in Lulu's–his mouth salivated at the thought.

"That girl, Rachel. Boss wants you to get her. Bring her to me tomorrow night."

"Why does the boss want Rachel?"

The Scotsman grabbed him by his jacket. "You don't think and you don't ask no fucking questions, you hear me? You get me that girl, you understand."

Gary nodded, his lips were quivering.

"There's a good lad."

"What about my partner? He won't let me just arrest her."

"Kill him. Who's gonna care about one dead cop? You've got the balls to do that, right?"

"S-sure, sure I can do it."

Donnie smiled. It was one of the scariest things Gary had ever seen.

19

He thought his head had hurt before, but it was nothing like the pain he felt now. Charlie rolled over and vomited down the side of the bench. The pain struck again, stabbing him behind the eyes and at the back of his neck. There was a ringing in his ears. He groaned and tried to remember where he was. The ringing persisted. It was then he felt his phone jostling him awake through his trouser pocket. Charlie checked the caller ID and pinched the bridge of his nose in frustration. It was Pinky Morris, the last person he wanted to deal with.

He considered letting it ring off. They weren't due to meet Pinky for another… he checked his watch and cursed. It was nearly noon. If he didn't take the call it would be as good as confessing to killing Pinky's men. He hit answer.

"Mr Morris," he said. "We were just getting ready to come over. I take it we're still on for today."

There was a pause, as though Pinky was contemplating his words carefully. "Change of venue, Mr Smith. I have a warehouse on the docks. Block four, number nine. Be there in an hour."

"Wait, a warehouse? You've got the money, right?"

"Don't be late." He hung up.

"Shit." Charlie put his head in his hands. What could be more inviting than a warehouse by the docks, with Pinky Morris picking out two pairs of concrete boots in their size? They would have to go, even when his head told him to run. Pinky suspected them now, and if he was smart he would already be trying to track them down. Even if they made it out of S'aven, how far would they actually get? He had no choice; he was running from too many people as it was.

Dialling John's number was harder than he expected. He loved his brother, but since Sarah's death their relationship was getting difficult. They weren't the type to sit down and talk, or offer manly hugs and words of encouragement. Much better to keep quiet, let things fester and corrode, that was the Smith way, tried and tested.

"Pinky's changed the time and the location," was all he said when John answered.

"Where?" John asked.

"The docks."

The silence said it all. "Great. When?"

"One hour. I'm not far."

"I'll meet you there. What about Rachel?"

"Keep her at the lockup."

John wouldn't ask what they were going to do afterwards. That decision was Charlie's, if his brother disagreed, well maybe that would be the moment their relationship broke down. There had been so many fights along the way and so few apologies. That would mean admitting fault, expressing feelings. It was easier to just pretend everything was fine, bandage up the old wounds and hope infection wouldn't set in. When it did he would let John go without a fuss. No drama, it was the least he could do. But when it happened, and he was sure it would, he had no idea how he would cope without his little brother watching his back.

They met at the edge of the docks, where the smell of fish and sea collided with the sulphuric fumes of the neighbouring factories. John stood like a tall mast protruding out of the harbour. When he made himself visible he was impossible to miss. Wrapped up in his thick black trench coat he was an immovable figure against the harsh breath of the ocean. He was immaculate, despite a night in the lockup, which was more than could be said for Charlie.

The elder brother hobbled forward like some kind of decrepit swamp creature. He stank of sweat and vomit and grime. There were stains down his coat, dirt clogged to the thick layer of stubble against his face. And he felt worse than he looked. He nodded at John, marking the start and end of their apologies.

"You armed?" Charlie asked.

"The usual." He had one pistol in his holster that they would find. One snub in his boot which was lazily concealed and a knife they would have to autopsy him to uncover. "Is there a plan?"

"Leave alive." *The best laid plans,* Charlie thought to himself.

"Sounds good."

They walked towards the warehouse as a united front.

There were goons and then there were trained professionals. Charlie had worked with enough gangsters to know that muscle was just dead weight. Even men as big as houses had no chance of getting one over on his brother. So, if he walked into the warehouse with a slight swagger to his stagger, he felt that he had justification. Only these men weren't goons. They were soldiers. Sure, their uniforms were just standard issue street armour but these men had seen conflict. Their eyes betrayed the cold, calculating nature of their violent lives. These men didn't have families, or morals, or hopes, or dreams. These men had orders, they lived on orders, they died on orders.

Charlie flicked his eyes across them. Fourteen men, two women, and a cage of dogs. It was overkill even against John. Charlie's confidence faltered. He stumbled forward. Hands reached out for him, holding him steady. Holding him still.

He turned into a fist, feeling his cheekbones crack on impact. As he hit the floor his back wailed in agony. Before he could catch his breath he was lifted into the air and smacked across the face again. His teeth sliced into his tongue and smashed against each other. Then a fist in his gut commandeered his thoughts. He dropped to his knees but had the foresight to throw a return punch. Whatever he hit, he hit it hard. His hand was in agony. He spat blood onto the floor and tried to stand. Where was the crutch? He reached out, but it was too late. The barrel of a sawn off shot gun was pressed to his head. There'd be nothing left of his skull when it went off.

"Mr Smith, that's enough."

Charlie thought it was directed at him and he was fairly happy to concede defeat. But the comments were meant for his brother. John stood, a gun outstretched in either arm, neither belonged to him. He had Charlie's assailant covered and every other barrel in the warehouse pointing his way. There were two men by his feet, and he didn't have a scratch on him.

John didn't take orders. He only really took suggestions from Charlie. He looked at his brother. After all, it was his brother's life hanging in the balance, it was only fair that Charlie decide what to do. Charlie gave him the *stick to the plan* nod and watched with relief as his brother lowered his weapons.

"You should keep your brother on a tighter leash, Charlie." Pinky Morris was unarmed; he wasn't even wearing a vest. He stood in the centre of the warehouse daring Charlie to do something about it.

The Running Game

"Guess we didn't expect such a warm welcome."

"Two of my men are dead."

It didn't matter that Pinky had his suspicions. Throwing punches and asking questions later was a lousy way to conduct business. Charlie's body was throbbing in places he'd forgotten could hurt. The agony in his back was overshadowed by something more pressing–he was pissed off. He wiped the blood from his mouth. It had already poured onto his coat.

"What the fuck is going on?" He growled, suddenly matching his brother in fierceness.

He got a foot in the back of his knee and dropped down. John twitched. A telltale sign someone was about to die. Charlie raised his hand. He could tolerate pain; this was nothing compared to trying to get out of bed in the middle of the night.

Pinky moved closer to Charlie, keeping his distance from John. He had Charlie lifted to his feet.

"Did you kill them?"

"Did we kill who?"

"My men?"

"Why would we kill your men?"

"You were with James Roxton last night."

"What's he got to do with anything?"

"I ask the questions."

He got another beating for his trouble.

"Okay! Yes, I bumped into Roxy. We had a couple of drinks. He's an old friend of ours. What the fuck does that have to do with anything? We just came for our money."

"Your services are no longer required."

Guns cocked in every direction. "You fucking bastard. We did a good job. Call yourself a fucking business man!"

Pinky's hand slapped Charlie across the face. Charlie spat more blood on the floor, spattering it over Pinky's shoes.

"When I do business, Charlie, I get what I want."

"We gave you what you wanted. We did everything you asked for. What's the matter, can't you afford it?" The punches barely hurt anymore.

"Your information was lousy. Kill them," he ordered.

Charlie lurched forward. "Bullshit! Our work was solid. You tell me what you want and I'll get it for you!"

"I want Rachel Aaron."

"We found her for you."

"And then my boys were killed."

"I don't know how your boy's were killed, but what if we bring you the girl, how about that? You give us our money, just what we agreed, and we get to live. How does that sound?"

Pinky paused, his tongue licking at his lower lip like he was tempted. Charlie could see the man was desperate; he wouldn't be toying with them like this if he wasn't, and all Charlie needed to do was make sure the bait was right.

"Give us a week. We'll track her, get her for you. We can do it. Hell, if we knew that was what you wanted we'd have done it for you straight away. It doesn't have to be like this."

Charlie knelt forward helplessly. "Please, Pinky. We need the money. We need it to find my little girl. As soon as we get paid we're out of here, heading for the North, you'll never see us again."

Pinky knelt down so he was level with Charlie, his heart strings seemingly un-pulled. "You bring her here in two days, Mr Smith, or I'll see to it that your priest compensates me personally for his bad recommendation."

Charlie ground his teeth, pressing into his already sore gums. This was not how good businessmen operated. Either Pinky didn't have the money or he was too stupid to hand it over. It didn't matter either way because after this, after the threats, the beatings, the total lack of hospitality, Charlie would take everything he could. He would take Rachel and the money and Pinky Morris would rue the day he decided to cross the Smith Brothers.

"We want our money," Charlie told him.

"Payment on completion of the job."

"He's bullshitting," John said. "He's not got the money."

"You boys aren't in a position to argue. And don't think about getting your priest out of the city. I've already got him under watch." Pinky smiled as though he had won. "Keep me posted, boys. Get them out of here!"

Charlie felt a tug at his collar before he was dragged from the warehouse. The soldiers were too smart to do the same to John. The entourage of gun barrels glared at him until he stepped free of the warehouse. Charlie retrieved his crutch, not that he needed it, he was so mad he wanted the pain to calm him down.

Blood was drying on his cheek. His knuckles stung from that one lucky punch. This was what life had been like. And he loved it.

"So?" John asked.

"So, that bastard is going to regret the day he decided to piss me off."

20

Rachel had held off for as long as she could but in the end she had to go.

She opened a crack in the door to the lockup and peered out. Heavy smog was settling into the maze of containers and garages surrounding her. She had no idea what time it was but the district was already pulsating with heavy machinery. Figures moved like ghosts throughout the mist, workers readying themselves for a hard slog, or trudging back home to sleep and starve.

Using an ornate brass jug to keep the door open, she slipped into the fog, pandering to the call of nature and looking for a discreet cranny she could slip into. It was easy to go unnoticed. She passed a group of shadows not even drawing a glance from them. She wondered what they actually saw when they looked at her. Was she a shade? Maybe she wasn't even there at all. Either way it worked, sometimes when she didn't even realise. Being part of the shadows was as natural to her as breathing in and out.

When she returned to the lock up the door was wide open. A flicker of excitement ran through her when she realised John and Charlie were back. Only it wasn't John or Charlie. It wasn't even Roxy. A man and a woman, wrapped in worn work clothes, were rummaging through the boxes. Rachel swallowed nervously. Her instinct was to leave them to it; there was nothing worth dying for in the lockup. But John wouldn't run and if she wanted to work with them she needed to think like them.

She stepped inside, hidden from them both. They were opportunists, looking for anything they might sell quickly and getting annoyed at the pointless spoils. Until their attention turned to the car. Rachel swore to herself, the keys were still in the ignition.

"What are we going to do with a car?" The woman snapped.

"I don't know, go somewhere?"

"Where we gonna go, huh?" She pushed his shoulder. "You can't even drive."

"We could sell it. I know a guy."

"What guy?"

The man pushed her back. "A guy I know. Reckon we might even get a hundred for it."

The woman's eyes lit up. Rachel stepped behind her.

"Not today," Rachel said as she unveiled herself.

They both leapt backwards, yelping like frightened puppies. It took the woman a moment to recover. She was obviously the driving force of their idle operation. She was bigger than Rachel, brimming with muscles from years of hard labour. Her face was black, her head shaven just like her friend.

"I counts two of us, sweetie-pie," the man said.

"See, darling, everything I said about these backwater inbred drones–not a brain cell between them." Roxy stepped into the lockup. He casually placed a tray of steaming paper cups on the car bonnet and then took in the intruders disapprovingly. "Can't even do simple maths. Let's try a question from left field to see if you can redeem yourself. If four people are standing in a lockup, how many guns do they have among them?"

The man caught on quicker. His jaw wobbled pathetically.

"We didn't mean nothing by it, the door was open," he babbled. "We's just hungry, looking for food is all, with winter coming. We don't want no trouble." He held up his hands, backing away towards the door.

Eventually the woman followed. Roxy waved at them as they went and then slammed the door shut.

"So, the door was open?"

"I needed to pee," Rachel said in her defence. "Would you rather I do it in the car?"

Roxy shrugged. "You could have closed the door."

"Then how would I get back in? I don't know what your problem is. It's not like there's anything in here worth stealing. I mean, the porn is so benign it's practically PG."

"Yeah well, buying pornography off the Samaritans wasn't my greatest idea," Roxy conceded. "But that doesn't mean you leave the door open. I might have something in here worth stealing and not even realise."

"I'm sorry," Rachel said, pathetically pouting at him. "I promise to never do it again."

Roxy waved his hand dismissively. It was already forgotten. "I liked the way you materialised out of nothing though, pretty sweet move there, pet."

She felt a pang of panic. Obviously he knew what she was, there would be no reason for Charlie to keep it a secret, but it was terrifying having him talk to her about it.

"With a talent like yours you're wasted in a deadbeat hospital. Hey, where's the handsome bodyguard?"

"He went to meet Charlie."

"That was very trusting of him, leaving you here all on your own."

"Why do you think he can't trust me?"

Roxy flashed a devilish grin at her. "I meant trusting me, sweetheart." He gave her a wink and then reached for a paper cup. "Here. I got you the works, with real cream and sugar."

She had tasted coffee once, when Mark brought home his spoils from a raid at the docks. Most of the officers grabbed a stash of coke, but not Mark, he grabbed one of the confiscated bags of coffee and totally forgot about the sugar. Rachel remembered the thick, bitter tasting tar burning the back of her throat and the heart palpitations that followed. She almost considered handing the coffee back to Roxy, but it was a commodity and it would have been rude not to drink it. Gingerly, she placed the coffee to her lips, dreading the sensation. Her mouth filled with creamy, syrupy liquid. When she pulled the cup away it was empty.

"Wow … that was nice."

Roxy handed her a paper bag. "Muffin?"

"Oh my God, where did you get these?"

"Didn't John tell you? I'm a magician."

She stuffed a muffin into her mouth whole. It had been more hours than she could remember since she last ate. Her stomach protested as the rich, sweet food started to tantalise a constitution built on protein bars and soya. She fought against it with another muffin. Any doubts she had about the crazy situation in which she found herself were obliterated with the blueberry that burst into her mouth. Real fruit! She hadn't tasted real fruit for months.

"This is amazing," she tried to say with her mouth bulging.

Roxy shrugged, pretending to be indifferent and failing. His eyes were animated and excited, clearly he was enjoying having an audience to impress and if that meant she could finish the bag of muffins by herself then she would happily indulge a show off. Roxy was an egotist, a man who lived only for himself. It didn't mean he would hurt her, or even try to cause her harm, but she would never be able to trust him. No matter how many cakes he bought, or how many times he flexed his broad muscles as he inspected his useless stock. No matter how much he pursed his thick lips or hummed in his soothing, suggestive tones, he was not reliable. Not like John. Not like Charlie.

"I wouldn't let it persuade you into a life of crime. It's not all fluffy cakes."

"It suits you."

"Everything suits me."

He had an infectious smile and when he looked at Rachel she felt like just the two of them were in on some secret joke. Quickly, she glanced away. He could not be trusted, pretty eyes or not.

"Question of course is: what would a little thing like yourself be thinking, joining forces with the beautiful but deadly Brothers Smith?"

"I want to live," she replied honestly.

Roxy started to laugh. "Then I repeat the question. Charlie doesn't have the best track record at keeping people alive."

"He'll look after me," she assured him.

"He couldn't look after his wife, what makes you think he'll be different with you?"

"Because of what happened to his wife. I know he will do everything in his power to keep me alive. John will too."

"How can you be so sure? We're criminals, not exactly the most trustworthy of people."

Rachel stepped forward; it was her turn to show off. "I'm a Reacher, all I had to do was touch Charlie and I could read his mind."

Roxy smirked mischievously. "Where'd you touch him?"

"I kissed him."

"You kissed Charlie?"

"It's the best way of reading someone's thoughts. Well not the best way, but it's intimate enough to tell me what I need to know. I kissed Charlie and I saw everything I needed to see."

"And what about John?"

"I had to be sure I could trust them both."

Roxy's face was dumbstruck. "Which was better?" He finally said.

Rachel shook her head and nudged him with her elbow. "None of your business."

He licked his lips. "So what about trusting me?"

"Trusting you?"

"Yeah, I mean, we're here, all alone. Don't you want to know if you can trust me?" He flexed his broad shoulders like some kind of stallion readying himself for a jump. It was a façade. Kissing her, even flirting with her, was something to pass the time. Roxy liked attention and he liked to have fun. That was why Charlie liked him and why John mistrusted him. Rachel found herself in a strange medium. She wanted to take a stance and found herself just staring at his thick lips and wondering how far out of her comfort zone she wanted to dive.

Eventually, she laughed at herself. "I wouldn't trust you as far as I could throw you."

"And you know this even without a little lip action?"

"You ooze dishonesty. I can smell it all over you."

Roxy leaned towards her. He was so close she could smell the coffee and tobacco on his breath. "Smells delicious, doesn't it." He gave her a winning look.

Rachel pursed her lips, certain that he wasn't going to get the upper hand on her, ever. She leaned in closer. "I'm sure it tastes even better."

His smugness faltered. There was a bang at the door and still he gawped at her. *Rachel: score one.*

The banging grew louder. Roxy rolled his eyes and backed away. He pressed himself against the door.

"Who is it?" He teased.

"Open the goddamn door!" John shouted back.

"What's the password?"

"I'm going to shoot you!"

"Now, that's not really an incentive to let you in."

"Damn it Roxy! Open the door!" Charlie demanded.

Roxy unlocked the door for John to kick open. Behind him Charlie staggered inside. His face was bruising with each shaky step. Before she could even ask what had happened John had grabbed Roxy.

"What the fuck have you done to Pinky Morris?" John looked close to mauling Roxy and this time Charlie wasn't stepping in to break them up.

"What makes you think I've done anything to that old bastard?" Roxy glanced at Rachel and winked. It was all just a big game.

But it wasn't, not for John, or for Charlie.

"How about that kiss, Roxy–then you won't have to tell us," she said. *Score two.*

He knew when he was beat. Roxy patted John's hands until his feet were set comfortably on the floor. His eyes flickered to each of them, full of innocence.

"Okay, I'll be straight with you. I may have lifted a few items that possibly, maybe, belonged to someone who could have been Pinky Morris. I guess he's pissed about it."

"You didn't think you should mention this to me?" Charlie said. It was only then Rachel saw the full damage to his face. He was in pain, more pain than usual. All his weight was balanced on his crutch and yet he wasn't wavering. It didn't make sense that he looked better than when she had last seen him, but he did.

"Honestly Charlie, it never even entered my head. I've ripped off most of S'aven. I don't think there's a guy you could work for who wouldn't be gunning for me." Roxy brushed off John's hands and smiled. "It's no big deal. We'll kiss and make up at some point. And speaking of kissing… how about it Rachel?"

John pushed him back, away from her. "If you're lying…"

"I know, I know. You'll hurt me in unimaginable ways. And after I brought you coffee and gave you a place to stay. Honestly John, sometimes I wonder if we're even friends."

"We're not."

Roxy sighed. "Well fine, I'll be on my way and you boys can find out all by yourselves why Pinky wants Rachel so bad." *Roxy score one,* Rachel thought.

The look that passed between the brothers was an old one. One cultivated through years of dealing with Roxy.

"You know?" Charlie leaned back on the car for support, curiosity was getting the better of him. It was getting the better of Rachel too.

"I did what you two should have done before you took this job. Asked around this morning. It didn't take a genius to figure it out. But if you don't want my help there are no hard feelings."

"Roxy," Charlie said as he reached for his lukewarm coffee and toasted his old friend. "As ever you have been a godsend. Any further help you can offer us would be so gratefully received we would be forever in your debt." Flattery: the best way to deal with him.

Roxy looked to John, waiting for a similar response.

"Just tell us or I will hurt you."

"With that kind of charm how can I resist? Now you may have heard of Pinky's departed brother the late Frank Morris. Back in the good old days Frank was the heart of the operation. Damn psychopath too. If you think Pinky is bad you should have seen what his brother was capable of.

"Anyway, Frank was at the top but he was totally paranoid about the people around him. Somehow he meets this girl, she was just a kid, not even in her teens. Then wherever Frank goes his girl follows. She lives in his house, goes to work. She spends more time with him than his goddamn girlfriends. As she gets a bit older she starts doing the rounds amongst the men. And suddenly snitches are ratted out, double crosses are pre-empted. Turns out this girl's a Reacher. She can read minds and she's working exclusively for Frank.

"For a while everyone in the city is terrified of Frank. They're even terrified of thinking about Frank in case the girl picks up on it. But the longer it goes on the more people start to lose their patience. Wouldn't you, having your head messed with all the time? At the same time Frank's pumping more and more money into finding Reachers. Business is going south and what's worse is his little girl is all grown up and happens to be taking an interest in one of Frank's boys. Guy by the name of Donnie Boom. There are lots of theories about the story, but basically Donnie gets pissed when he finds out that Frank has more than fatherly intentions towards the girl and maybe she is more than compliant. Whatever the case, he waits until they're out for a romantic meal together and blows them both into tiny pieces. Leaving Pinky Morris to clean up what's left of Frank's mess, both literal and figurative."

Roxy leaned against the car allowing the suspense to build. "Rachel, don't suppose you happened to have an older sister."

Rachel closed her eyes. As soon as he had mentioned the girl she knew he was talking about Isobel. The girls were six and nine, fleeing the outbreak of yet another rebellion in Red Forest when they managed to find their father's friend, an old priest who took them in. In the weeks that followed the girls were split up and Rachel was sent to hide in a convent while Isobel remained in S'aven. Rachel had been devastated at the separation; it had been like losing a part of herself. But then the years went by and the emptiness she felt eased, even if it didn't really heal. She wrote to Isobel and received long letters from her older sister boasting about her socialite lifestyle and slowly the emptiness was replaced with envy. By the time Rachel set off for S'aven, leaving the convent for good, her sister and her sister's life was an exciting mystery to her.

A decade of absence separated the girls and Rachel wasn't stupid enough to think that the Isobel she had left had remained unchanged in that time. She certainly hadn't so why would her sister be different? When the convent closed and she fled back to S'aven she'd been excited but also apprehensive about finding her sister. Apart from seeing their father gunned down in the woods, the memories Rachel had from her time before the convent were hazy at best. She could only just remember her sister's face as she stood beside the old priest, watching as Rachel left S'aven. They shared powers, they shared a difficult, lonely journey across the country, but after that they were strangers.

"Seems your sister had the talent to make Frank Morris a very powerful man. I'd say his deadbeat brother has latched onto a similar notion. He always was the less inspired brother."

It was unsettling hearing Roxy talk about her, as though somehow she should have found all this out already and that she had let Isobel down by abandoning her search for answers when she first arrived in S'aven and discovered Isobel had been killed.

"Her name was Isobel," Rachel said. It was strange to say the name after so long.

"Did you know she was dead?" Charlie asked, settling beside her.

Rachel nodded, remembering the moment she felt her sister pass. "I'd just arrived in the city. We'd always shared a connection and then one day it just stopped and I knew. It was an explosion?" she asked Roxy.

"Killed them both instantly," Roxy told her.

It was such a long time ago that Rachel was surprised she still felt a pang in her chest. Charlie's hand touched her shoulder.

"I need some air," he murmured. "Can you give me a hand?"

Just as she sensed his grief, he immediately picked up on hers. She helped him out into the open smog, but as the door closed he was supporting her. She wiped the unexpected tears that had somehow slipped from her eyes.

"Sorry," she whispered, feeling foolish. "I don't even know why I'm crying."

"It sneaks up on you, believe me."

"Yeah, but it's been seven years." She tried to get herself together. "We weren't that close. I mean we were separated when we were kids. I always thought she'd got the better deal. She got to come to the city while I was stuck in a convent. God, I thought she was happy, I felt like she was having a good time, but they were making her…" She couldn't bring herself to say it. Her sister, her beautiful sister, forced to whore herself out when she was so young.

"We wrote to each other all the time. Never specifics in case anyone ever found the letters, but enough. I remember writing to her, telling her I had a job at St Mary's. I told her I'd got a job at Mum's hospital. Mum's name was Mary. She was so excited, she was going to meet me once I got settled. We had to be careful, two Reachers in one city would have been dangerous. And then I got here and two days later I felt her go. It was so quick."

"And you were stuck in S'aven," Charlie added.

"I didn't think it'd be that bad, but it was just like the convent. I was in another prison, just on a bigger scale, with more dangerous inmates."

"What about where you sent the letters to?"

"We never had an address for each other. The nuns delivered all of our letters. It was safer that way. And we'd destroy them as soon as we read them."

"Not your last letter," Charlie informed her. "Pinky Morris has it. I didn't know you were writing to your sister. He gave it to us so we could track you down."

Rachel sighed. "So that's how he found out about me."

Charlie reached for her hand and she felt the connection between them getting stronger. She was unsure of what lay ahead and that made her afraid, but she was angry too. There was a burning inside of her that matched his own. He couldn't stop her, even if he wanted to. She was going to put a stop to Pinky Morris. With their hands linked she knew that he sensed all this and that the only thing he could do was try to keep her alive.

"I'm sorry about last night," he murmured. "I just needed to clear my head."

And he needed a fix. It went unsaid, but Rachel understood.

"I appreciate where you were coming from. It's nice to have someone watching my back."

"Yeah, well, I said what I said because I'm a selfish bastard. I can't have another death on my conscience."

"Then I'll do my best to stay alive."

"Are you serious about this? Me and John come with a health warning. If you stay with us you'll be in the same firing line. There are people, worse than Pinky..." He paused. "There'll be no going back."

She smiled. "I have nothing to go back to."

"Okay then, welcome to the team," he shook her hand with a painful smirk.

His face was now nicely purple and swollen. "Jesus, Charlie you look like shit, what exactly happened to you guys?" She said hoping to change the subject at least while she got her emotions in check

As though he had forgotten about the pain, he touched his swollen lip and winced. "We had a disagreement with Pinky's men."

"You took them on alone?"

Charlie glanced away sheepishly, "No, John was there too."

"But there's not a mark on him."

"Yeah tell me about it."

"Does it hurt?"

He gave her a look–of course it hurt.

"Give me your hands," she demanded and from her tone he knew not to argue.

The sensation when they touched was like dipping their hands in warm water. Rachel's hands grew warmer. She closed her eyes, her brow furrowed in concentration. Slowly she felt the pain in Charlie's body start to ease. The nagging agony in his face, his back, all of it seemed to sigh into a dull, manageable ache.

Rachel opened her eyes. "Pain is basically a signal being sent to your brain. You get hit in the face and your nerves start screaming at your brain. The trick is to tell your brain it doesn't hurt."

"And that's what you're doing?"

She released him. "How do you feel?"

He thought about it. "Better."

"It works on other things too. You saw the kid at the hospital. He went away because I gave his brain a fix."

He looked away embarrassed. She reached out and squeezed his shoulder.

"We can sort it out, Charlie. I can get you back to what you were. I can help you get your daughter back."

Roxy and John were still arguing inside the lockup. Charlie stepped in the garage, fighting the limp and staying upright. He was stronger, despite the bruises. He coughed and both men quieted down. This was how it used to be, before the world ended. Rachel stood by his side. It felt right.

"We're going to take everything Pinky wants. We've got two days. Are you in, Roxy?"

"Would I pass up the chance to piss off that wanker? Count me in. I take it we have a plan?"

Charlie Smith, Mr Can-Do-Anything-Just-Try-And-Stop-Him, smiled. He was back.

21

The best plans take time and patience. Neither of which they had. Charlie had to go on what he knew. They weren't going to take everything, just what they could reach in two days. Pinky's eyes would be on finding Rachel, so he'd never see them coming until it was too late. But first he had to make a stop.

Charlie gripped the dashboard as John took another corner without hitting the brakes. His brother was brooding and had been since they'd left Rachel alone with Roxy. Roxy's presence had always added tension to their work, which wasn't surprising. He was infuriating, untrustworthy, and went out of his way to piss John off every chance he got. But when he was given a job, even if it was the shittiest job on the mission, Roxy would get it done. And, although he gave the impression he'd screw anything that moved, he was actually a gentleman, and Charlie was pretty sure Rachel could take care of herself even if he did try it on.

Another corner and Charlie's stomach lurched.

"Why don't you just drive us into the next wall and get it out of your system?" He yelled at his brother.

John flipped up his finger in response.

"Look, we need Roxy."

The look he got was venomous.

"You can pull that face all you want; you know we did our best work with him. And he's our friend John."

"We can't trust him. He's sold us out before."

"That was a long time ago. You can't keep bringing it up every time you want him off a job. Roxy saved my life, he was part of our operation right up until Sarah's death. And yeah, okay, he got sticky fingers now and again, but he's a thief, that's just his nature. He never put any of us in danger, not like we did. Look there's nothing in this job for him, even if there was he knows the money is for finding Lilly, he'd never screw her over."

"If there's nothing in it for him why's he helping us?"

"Because, as much as you hate to admit it, we are not the only two people who care about getting Lilly back!" Charlie had raised his voice louder than he had intended. "There was a time when Roxy was as good as family, and maybe he is an asshole and would rob us in our sleep if he got half a chance but he knows this is more than business."

A silence fell between the brothers. Charlie sighed, sometimes John was impossible. He forgot that Roxy had been the only one he could turn to when he needed to break Charlie out of hospital. He forgot that Roxy got them out of London.

Another corner and it was clear John wasn't going to back down. The younger brother gripped the steering wheel as though it was trying to escape. His jaw was twitching in frustration.

"Come on, I thought you'd be happy we're doing the job. And if he does anything wrong I promise you can shoot him," Charlie finally said.

John slowed the car and Charlie felt that he'd made amends until he realised they were pulling up outside the ramshackle church Father Darcy had made his home.

"Can you see anyone around?"

There was no point in looking himself, if anyone was there John would spot them long before he made out a shadow.

"We're clear. Maybe Pinky was bluffing."

"Or maybe he doesn't travel at the speed of light like you do," Charlie added. "I'll meet you back at Rachel's. Roxy said Fat Joe is the one to question about the money. You sure you can get everything we need?"

John took offence. "Are you sure you can get across the road without a hand?" He sneered. "Of course I can. Give me two hours, and he'll be singing Pinky's bank account numbers in stereo."

"All right, just be careful. We don't..." Charlie stopped when John's hands clenched the steering wheel even tighter. "Okay, okay. I'll see you later."

John's foot was on the accelerator before Charlie closed the door. He was keen to get on the job, but even keener to get away from the church. Darcy had looked after them both when they were kids, but John had always been uncomfortable in the old priest's presence. He was intimidated by religion and righteousness. Even waiting outside the church was a challenge. Charlie wasn't a religious man himself, but Sarah had been raised a Catholic. Through her Charlie had always been able to appreciate the faith and the dedicated men like Darcy who continued to preach long after the government reclaimed the right to God.

There were no churches in the city. No temples, no synagogues, or mosques. No religion. But in the nooks and crannies there were ramshackle huts where people of faith could gather. The government called it plotting, but most of the time they'd just sit and pray. Darcy had been moved across the country, even serving time in the work camps when the government had nowhere else to put him. The latest church was in the basement of an old public library. The rooms above had been overrun by wounded soldiers with nowhere else to go now that they were no use to the country. It was a stronghold for Darcy; the soldiers would protect him against the cops and for a while at least his work could continue.

Soldiers sat on the main stairs to the old library. Old veterans smoked with young amputees, trading war stories and contemplating the futility of it all. Charlie hobbled past and they tipped their heads to him as though he was one of their own. A twist of stairs dipped down below the pavement. Charlie took a deep breath and readied himself for twelve steps of agony.

The chapel was just a room. Assorted chairs and benches were lined up in front of a makeshift altar. The service was over, but one man remained, chatting with Father Darcy, holding a bottle in his hand. The church goer was obviously a soldier. He was missing half the red hair on his pink head, his eye was blinded white and the war had torn apart most of his left side. Charlie's back was still burning from his battle with the stairs, but he was already feeling like a fraud. The wars exploding around Europe were tiny factions of hell leaking out into the world. Charlie had passed through one two years before Sarah had died and vowed to never do it again. He had nothing but respect for the men and women who continued to fight, even when what they were fighting for was lost somewhere between the empty shells and human tissue.

Father Darcy had waded through more wars than any of the men above him. He preached on his knees to avoid bullets. He sat in infirmaries comforting the dying. Despite the things he had seen Darcy was always smiling, flashing a mouth of gaps and yellow teeth. His eyesight was failing and he always wore his thick glasses, taped together at the sides. Charlie had seen pictures of him with a thick afro but his hair had started to fall out in his thirties, now all that remained was grey fuzz, thinning over his head. He spotted Charlie and rose. Charlie stifled a laugh. The old priest was wearing a red and blue jumper, with a crude yellow star knitted towards the left of it. Another token from one of his beloved followers.

"Charlie?" Darcy rasped.

"Is this a bad time?" Charlie had no intention of waiting, but manners were important.

The soldier stood up and shook Darcy's hand. "I'll get out of your hair." He said in a thick Scottish accent and handed Darcy the bottle. "Thanks for your help, Father."

"Thank you for this. Are you sure you won't share it?"

"Try to stay away from the stuff, prefer to keep a clear head." The soldier tapped his skull and turned to Charlie. "Sorry mate, I'll leave you gents to it."

Charlie smiled gratefully. He stepped forward, drawing the soldier's attention.

"Where'd you serve?" He asked Charlie.

"London Central," Charlie replied.

"Sorry, I thought you were a soldier."

"Oh but Charlie is a soldier. A soldier of God," Darcy said proudly.

Charlie rolled his eyes. "Yeah something like that."

"Nice to meet you anyway," the Scotsman said awkwardly and shuffled past Charlie to get out of the church.

"You know I wish you wouldn't do that," Charlie told the priest once they were alone.

"And I wish you'd stop denying it. When God spoke to me he told me you were his angels, Charlie, you and your kind are destined for great things."

"Yeah well the rest of the world doesn't think that and if I remember the story right, you'd had at least two bottles of that before God started talking to you."

Darcy rapped Charlie across the back of the head. "Don't blaspheme and open this for me." He pushed the bottle into Charlie's hands. "Damn arthritis, I swear it's the devil."

Charlie opened the bottle and handed it back to him. The soldier had managed to get some pretty expensive booze. Charlie was impressed, all he'd brought Darcy was bad news.

"I didn't expect to see you. Young John not with you?"

"I think he's afraid he might spontaneously combust if he enters a House of God."

Darcy laughed and sipped from the bottle. He gestured that they sit down underneath the large crucifix hanging on the wall. *No one can hide from God.* That was always Darcy's motto. Sometimes Charlie thought he was made to sit there just so Darcy knew he was telling the truth.

"If you're still here I take it so is the girl?"

This was the moment Charlie was dreading. He hated standing up to Darcy. He'd rather stand up against God, He was less vengeful. "She's staying with us."

"You think your life is better than a life at the convent?"

"No, but she does. She won't let us take her to safety. In fact, she outright refuses. We figured our only option was keeping her with us."

"She's important, Charlie, and your work–your work is violent and dangerous."

"This world is violent and dangerous. Darcy, I'm not going to force her to go anywhere she doesn't want to. She's a grown woman, she can think for herself. And she's tough, even managed to impress John. But that's not why I'm here."

Darcy sat back in his chair. For an eighty-year-old his movements were lucid and effortless. It filled Charlie with envy.

"Pinky Morris has threatened to kill you if we don't bring him Rachel."

"You must not give her to him, Charlie."

"Of course I'm not going to let him have her. Jesus, what do you think I am?"

"Jesus knows exactly what you are," Darcy replied.

Charlie sighed to himself. He used to argue theology with the priest, now it was easier to just let the comments slide. "I just came to give you a heads up. Pinky Morris has our money and because of his behaviour I've decided to charge interest. Things are going to get messy. You might want to think about moving on."

"There is more to this life than money."

"This isn't about money. We were going to work the job for the pittance that was offered, but Pinky Morris isn't going to let us walk away, or Rachel for that matter. This has to happen."

Darcy's brow lowered as if the very effort of thinking about Charlie's intentions were weighing him down. "This is a dangerous game you insist on playing, Charlie. Wouldn't it be better to just run?"

"That's what the game is, Darcy. We run and we're chased. The trick to surviving is making sure you have taken enough away from your enemies before they come after you. I've got to get back. We probably won't get chance to see you for a while."

"I understand. Take care of the girl, Charlie. If anything happens to her…"

Charlie nodded. "Will you leave the city?"

"Not quite yet. My work here is still unfinished. Don't you worry about me. I've got a whole army in the room upstairs." Darcy chuckled to himself as he reached out and clutched Charlie's arm. "I mean it, Charlie. Look after her for me, please."

"I promise you nothing will happen to her while I'm breathing." And he intended to stay breathing for as long as possible.

* * *

Donnie walked away from the church. He took the first corner and stopped to make a call.

"Boss, it's me. Charlie Smith has just shown up at the church."

"Did you give my message to the priest?"

"I told him if he wanted his secret kept he'd make sure the Smith Brothers brought you the girl."

Donnie waited for the dial tone and made his second call.

"Gary, it's me. Are we ready for tonight?"

22

Rachel opened the door to her old flat. It was almost exactly as she had left it, complete with a sink full of dirty dishes. Twenty-four hours had changed everything in her life, but not this place. This would never change.

"You live here?" Roxy said, pushing her aside to inspect the square room in amusement.

"I lived here," Rachel corrected under her breath. She ran her fingers over the unmade bed.

"It's…" Roxy grasped for the right word, clicking his fingers. "Enchanting."

"Screw you. I suppose you live in a mansion."

He wandered about the room, scrutinising the little that was there. Rachel was about to object until she realised there was nothing in the flat worth looking at. At least she didn't think there was.

"Please tell me these are yours," he said holding up a pair of boxers.

"Not my size," Rachel replied.

"So what, they belong to a casual passer-by? Evening trade? Long lost brother?"

"They're my boyfriend's."

Roxy fell back on the bed, groaning as his back hit the bed slats in the bare bits of mattress. "Don't you mean ex-boyfriend?"

Rachel shrugged. "Probably not for another week or so, when he gets hungry and realises I've actually gone."

"Is he another doctor?"

"Charlie didn't tell you? Mark's a cop."

Roxy sat up. His face flitted between disturbed and hysteria. "A cop?"

"A cop."

"A cop?"

"Yes."

"Living here?"

"Yes."

"With you?"

"Jesus, Roxy, do you want me to write it down for you? I live with a cop."

Roxy sucked in a breath, his eyes wide with wonder and amusement. He looked like he was ready to unleash another onslaught of repetitive questions but held it in.

"A cop?" He shook his head. "I knew they were stupid, but seriously, one has been living with a Reacher for how long?"

"Four years," she said and waited for another wave of disbelief.

"You're either really good or he is yokel dumb."

Rachel smiled. "I'd say it's half and half."

There was nowhere else to sit but the bed. She slumped down beside him. The dip in the mattress pressed them together. Her hand brushed his. His pulse was racing with adrenaline. He was excited, nervous, and brimming with energy. He was like a drug addict, but his blood was clean. His habit was danger and he was just getting stuck into a whole heap of trouble and he loved it. She reached her fingers out further, curious to unravel him a little. He shifted his body away from her, but leaned his face closer. His lips dallied around hers. He thought she wouldn't be able to resist him. But Rachel wasn't so easily conquered.

"You know there are more interesting ways to find out all my secrets," he murmured.

She tilted her head slightly. "I already touched you, what makes you think I don't already know them?"

He scowled, uncertainty written all over his face. She patted his leg. "Don't worry. I won't tell a soul."

Roxy smirked as he realised it was a bluff. "You might be just what those brothers actually need. It's about time they were taught humour."

"What are you talking about? John's a laugh a minute."

"That he is. What is it they say about him? You will know him by the trail of laughing corpses."

"I guess he got the looks and Charlie got the charm."

Roxy scoffed at the suggestion. "Charm? That motherfucker couldn't charm if he was dangling off a necklace."

"What's your problem with Charlie?"

"I don't have a problem with him."

It was Rachel's turn to scoff. "Bullshit. John treats you like crap, but it's Charlie you're cold with."

"As you said, John's prettier to look at. Much prettier these days. Charlie really has let himself go."

Rachel folded her arms. "Spill it."

"No."

"I'll touch you again."

"Do I get to pick where?"

"I'll grab your hand and every dark thought you've got rattling around in there will be mine." It was a lie. At best she'd be able to induce a headache.

He hesitated. The truth was clearly festering inside him and he squirmed in his seat as though it was taking every effort to hold it in. "Charlie's a selfish bastard, always has been." Roxy's mouth twitched, his mask slipped, and as the emotion escaped he couldn't hide from himself. "He stole my girlfriend, my best friend in all the world, married her, and then ended up getting her killed."

"Then why work with him?"

"Because he's the best. You can count on him when you're on a job, just not when you're sitting at home looking after his kid, it would seem."

"You know he relives it every day. He's in hell," Rachel told him. "I read his mind and there was nothing but pain."

"Good, he deserves it."

Rachel decided to let it drop. He wasn't going to change his mind about Charlie, at least not anytime soon. Roxy's composure was still low. He played with a cigarette in deep thought. Rachel got a feeling that his low times were tough, and she wasn't in a charitable mood to spend the next hour watching him mope.

She nudged him in the elbow. "Come on, then. I figure we've got half an hour, we might as well do it."

"Do it? What are you, twelve?" He started to laugh. Whether it was his normal self, or just the suit he wore, he was now smiling with ease. He leaned back on the bed and groaned again. "Fine, but if we're going to *do it* you're going to have to find a better bed. I've been in more comfortable fights than this."

Roxy fidgeted and grumbled until Rachel couldn't put up with it any more. She went to do the dishes before she killed him. She emptied out the sink, remembering the endless days of chores after a twelve hour shift. Roxy hummed behind her, drawing her back to reality. Soon Charlie and John would be back and this old life would be gone forever. A smile touched her face. She hummed back.

23

Riva and Pinky had been up all night. Neither one spoke. There wasn't a lot left to say. The room Riva had reserved for Rachel was empty. Two of their men were dead. And Donnie was still lurking in their shadow. He unsettled Riva, he always had. He had a way of looking at her, as though he were peeling the skin from her bones with just his eyes. Now he'd been in her house. The alarm was intact. There were no broken windows or picked locks. It meant he could do it again.

And it was clear now that Donnie wasn't on their side. He hadn't come back home, he'd come back to find the girl, and he'd used Pinky to get her. Pinky sat at their breakfast bar, picking strands of dead skin from his fingers. His eczema was back, stretching over his hands and arms, turning them bright pink and flaky. He ground his teeth, glaring at the marble floor, impatiently waiting for it to throw back answers. His blood pressure was up again. It had been since he'd learned of Rachel, and it wouldn't go down until they had her locked upstairs out of the way.

"Have you thought about paying the Smith Brothers?" She said, finally breaking the silence. "You could use men like them on your side while Donnie is still in the picture."

"They know too much," he stated.

"They know she's a girl, that's it. Pinky, honey, you need to protect yourself and the business. We need people we can rely on. They didn't know Izzy, they're not likely to put two and two together."

Pinky slammed his hand against the bar. "But Roxy knew. Who's to say he didn't tell them? Who's to say they didn't kill Jackie Walters?"

"They were at the bar that night," she assured him. "You're beginning to sound like Frank!"

He'd never hit her before. In all their married life, in all their feuds, and God knows there were a lot of them, he had never raised his hand to her. When it slapped across her cheek they were both surprised. It didn't hurt; at least the impact didn't. What Riva felt was deeper and more damaging than the slap alone. She thought about hitting him back, twice as hard, with something solid.

He stared at her, hatred burning in the back of his eyes. He looked like his brother. The brother who used to hit girls for fun. The brother who handcuffed a whore to his car door and drove off. The brother who made a little girl fuck all of his friends and learn their secrets.

"You've got a whole army of men at your disposal now. Get them here to guard this house. I don't want anyone getting in here again!"

She tried to face him. She was a strong woman, but her legs were shaking. "You touch me again," she quaked.

He grabbed her then, squeezing her arms so tight she cried out. "You'll what? Go crying to Pablo–oh, I forgot."

This isn't him, she told herself. *This isn't the man I love.*

"Get your men guarding this house tonight!" He tossed her back.

He made to leave and stopped himself. When he glanced back at her he seemed confused, like he didn't know where he was. His fingers scratched at the dead skin on his arms.

"I'm tired, I'm going to bed," he said softly.

As he left Riva cried. They just needed the girl, then everything would be all right. She had to make sure they got the girl.

24

"Well hurry, darling, we miss you," Roxy hung up on Charlie. "He's on the way," he told Rachel.

A key was pressed into the door.

"That was quick."

Rachel gasped. "Oh crap–it's Mark."

The door was clumsily pushed open. Mark lumbered in with his usual dopey smile. He was always so pleased to be home, as though the tiny room they lived in was something of a comfort. When he saw Rachel his face lit up, delighted they finally had a moment together. Then the other man in the room attracted his peripheral vision. Rachel watched his face morph as his brain slowly processed the scene. Surprise, confusion, suspicion. Mark gawped, his mind unable to assemble words. Rachel closed her eyes waiting for the fallout.

"Officer." The commanding tone to Roxy's gravelly voice surprised her. She opened her eyes and he looked like a totally different man. He'd pushed his hair back, was standing tall, his shoulders wide. He dominated the space around him as a man of authority would. He reached out for Mark's hand, blithely ignoring Rachel. "Hope you don't mind me dropping by like this, Mark, disturbing you and your lady here."

Mark shook his vacant head, he had no idea what was going on, and now neither did Rachel.

"Eh, no. Eh, who are you?" Mark asked.

Roxy looked genuinely offended. "You don't recognise me from the station?" He pulled out a leather wallet and flashed him an ID card—a police card. Rachel couldn't believe it.

"Special Agent Black, State Security. So I take it your staff sergeant didn't tell you I was coming?" Roxy sighed in despair. "No wonder this city is falling apart, I specifically asked that they contact you."

"No sir, nobody spoke to me." Mark gulped, he looked afraid.

"Imbeciles. So you have no idea why I'm here?"

"No, sir."

"Don't look so worried," Roxy laughed. "Or do you have something to be worried about?"

"Eh, no sir."

"Good. We've been watching your work, Mark and, well, we're impressed. Good officers are difficult to find and we need men that we can trust now more than ever."

The fear in Mark's face was transforming. This visit was what he'd been hoping for. All those extra shifts, someone had finally noticed him.

Rachel was frowning so hard her head started to hurt. Mark was buying the whole scam. If he looked, really looked, it was obvious Roxy wasn't the police. But he was selling an idea, one Mark wanted to believe above all else, and somehow it was working.

"Eh, thank you," Mark said.

"So we've cleared it with your boss. For this week you're off patrol and working for us. We have an important job for you but this stays between us, Mark. No going back to the station, no communication with anyone but me. Can you do that, officer?"

Mark's lip wobbled. Rachel pinched the bridge of her nose. It was getting painful to watch.

"This could be the making of you, son. Most people would kill for an opportunity like this." Roxy looked him up and down, weighing him up, judging his capabilities. "Now I need you in casual clothes, dark clothes."

"Eh, I don't have…"

Roxy waved his hand, "All right then, you'll have to buy some. You'll be staking out the place for a week, so bring provisions. Keep the receipts, we'll reimburse you. And pick up a phone too. Do not give the number to anyone but me, understand?"

Roxy handed him a card. "My number is on the back. Now there's an empty warehouse on the industrial estate. Block four, number eight. Be there at eight o'clock sharp. Do not be late and make sure you're not seen. I'll brief you on the particulars there."

Mark was still gawping.

"Do you understand, officer?"

Mark nodded. "Yes, sir." He glanced up at Rachel as though this were the most incredible moment of his life.

"Good, what are you waiting for then?"

"Right, of course." Mark looked to Rachel trying to offer her some kind of explanation but understanding nothing of what was happening. His face was reverberating with trepidation. Rachel gave him a nod of encouragement. It was all she could muster, knowing how devastated he would be when he realised he had been conned.

Mark turned back to the special agent. "Eh, are you coming?"

Roxy laughed at his naivety, playing the part like a pro. "Once I've had a chat with your girl here. Need her to be sure of a few points regarding the Secrecy Act. I'll check in with your sergeant too and let him know I've made contact with you. Remember, you're on radio silence until further notice. Looking forward to working with you, Mark."

He forced another handshake, guiding Mark out of his own flat. The door was slammed shut. Rachel waited for Mark to come to his senses. A few paces away from Roxy's charm surely he'd realise it was all a scam. He didn't. The man had a weakness for half brain ideas. She felt a pang inside her chest. He didn't deserve this.

"Why the hell did you do that?" She shoved Roxy in the shoulder.

There were so few cops in the city who actually cared, and even with his misguided, illogical, nonsensical, downright ridiculous ideas about the world, Mark was one of the good guys. But after all this, who knew what it would do to him.

Roxy shrugged nonchalantly. Rachel could see that in his eyes a cop was a cop. What did he care? "Gets him out of our hair, doesn't it?"

"When he doesn't show up to work he's going to get fired."

"Well, if you don't like it go after him and tell him it was all a lie." Roxy folded his arms, knowing full well there was nothing she could do, even if she wanted to. "If he knew what you were do you honestly think he wouldn't turn you in? This city is filled with scum and cops are the worst of the lot."

"Mark's not like that. He genuinely believes in the force."

"Then he's an idiot."

She couldn't argue with that so she pouted at him instead.

"You know honest cops tend to get murdered by their peers. I've probably just saved his life."

"You're an asshole," she replied.

"Well what I lack in manners I make up for in humour and handsomeness." He beamed. "Hey, what have you got to eat in this place?"

As he went to inspect the cupboards his mobile sounded off. The first bars of an Andy Williams song sounded.

"Hello?" He said, wedging the phone to his ear. "Well hello, my darling."

He glanced at Rachel and smiled. She was too angry to dignify him with a response.

"Anything for you, sweetheart." He hung up the phone and returned to the cupboard.

"Are you always such a smooth talker?" Rachel asked.

"If you must know, that was my mother. She expects it. My God, this really is dire. Let's get takeout. I know a great Chinese place."

"Didn't Charlie say we should wait here?"

Roxy scratched the mop of hair on his head. "And if he showed up and we were gone I suppose he'd probably do something rash and stupid. Tell you what, I'll be gone half an hour tops. You sit tight and I will get us a banquet!"

"What if someone comes?"

"Use your powers. Honestly, it'll be worth it. You ever had Chinese?"

She shook her head.

"In that case I'll get the works." He kissed the top of her forehead. "Here, take my phone. If anything goes wrong call John."

25

Gary had never killed anyone.

He'd let men be killed and he'd watched a guy hang himself from the level crossing bridge, but he'd never actually done the deed himself. Sometimes he fantasised about it, wrapping his hands around a neck, squeezing a bit harder than normal. Truth was he didn't have the nerve.

He'd promised the scarred Scotsman, damned if he could remember the guy's name, that he could do whatever was needed and the lie was starting to nag at him. Would he actually be able to kill his partner? He contemplated it over and over again as he watched Mark hurry towards the tramlines.

No matter how hard he tried he couldn't do it. He liked the kid. He was a good partner; didn't ask too many questions and he had Gary's back. Knowing Gary's luck he'd get paired with one of those do-good officers if he lost another partner. Then he wouldn't be able to work for Pinky at all. No, he couldn't do it. There had to be another way to get Rachel, he just had to be smart about it.

"Gary?" Mark said as he crossed the road. "You okay? You were just staring off at nothing."

"I'm good. You heading home?"

"Eh, no." Mark fidgeted with his hands. He always reminded Gary of his youngest son, squirming whenever he was trying to keep a secret.

"Don't tell me we've been called back to the station. God damn, that's fucking out of order! We do eight hours on the beat and they don't even give us fucking time to take a piss."

"I'm not going down to the station. Listen, I'm not supposed to say anything, but I'm working with Special Forces this week."

There were moments in Gary's life when he felt the world kick him in the gut. The wind would suddenly be taken out of him in an unprovoked assault. This was one of those times. Special Forces was interested in his partner–his partner who had been working the streets for four measly years. His partner who could count the number of arrests he had ever made on his fingers alone. And where was Gary? Stuck walking the beat, edging closer and closer towards retirement without a senior officer pay-off. There was a conspiracy somewhere. The lingering pacifism was over. If he could have, he would have shot Mark dead and there would have been no regrets.

"You can't tell anyone, okay? I didn't even get a chance to talk to Rachel. The agent just showed up at the flat and told me to get going. I don't think she has a clue what's going on."

This was it. Gary was growing hungry. He licked at his lips. "I'll talk to her if you like."

"Oh, would you, man? That would put my mind at rest."

"She at home?"

"Yeah, I don't think she has a shift until the morning."

The images circling Gary's thoughts were mesmerising. He could picture Rachel on her knees. She would be sobbing so hard, bruises forming on her face. She'd tell him she was sorry for all those disgusted looks, she'd beg him to do her again and again and when he was done he'd hand her over to Pinky Morris, collect his reward and watch Mark's world fall apart.

26

The back door to Riva's was unlocked.

Roxy slipped inside and headed for the basement. Nobody saw him. Riva was already there, chewing on a false nail impatiently. She was wearing more makeup than usual, more than she ever needed to. The thick layers of foundation were darker on her left cheek – a bruise. It wasn't like her to sport injuries like that.

"Riva, you look as lovely as ever," he lied. A part of him debated whether he should bring the bruise up.

She raised her finger to stop him speaking. "We're going to cut to the chase, Roxy. I know you know what's going on. I know you're working with the Smith Brothers, and I know you have access to the girl."

Roxy smirked in amusement. Riva always was the sharp one in the Morris family; it was her business savvy that had kept Pinky afloat for all these years, after all.

She sidled closer to him, tempting him with forbidden promises. Her fingers entwined around the empty button holes in his jacket. "I also know how much you want Donnie Boom."

* * *

John got into the car and wiped the blood stains off his fist with a bacterial wipe. Fat Joe was unconscious, tied up, and wedged into his bathtub. He'd live, or rather he wouldn't die of his injuries. A sudden fatty clog in his arteries could finish him off at any moment, but John wasn't prepared to take responsibility for anything like that.

It was funny, Fat Joe was the money man because he could be trusted. He liked his food, his TV, and doing Sudoku in his underwear on the couch. There was no ambition, no threat, and no nasty habits that would give him sticky fingers. He was Pinky's perfect employee; at least he would be if he wasn't such an easy target. Unfortunately for Joe, his lack of anything but an enthusiasm for custard donuts had made him slow and weak. John had overpowered him in seconds and after cracking one rib, Joe was singing every tune on request.

In fact, John got the impression that Joe wanted to talk. Maybe he only took the light beating to cover his back. Whatever the case it didn't matter. Now John knew where the money was. Fifty thousand, plus the takings from yesterday. If that didn't make Charlie happy nothing would.

He started the car and went to pick up his brother.

27

An actual meal, with real meat and vegetables; it sounded amazing. Rachel had to admit it, she was getting stupidly excited about a night off, gorging herself on good food, without having to deal with Mark or work in the morning. So far the luxuries were far outweighing the danger in this new life with the Smith Brothers. For the first time, in as long as she could remember, she sprawled out on her bed and switched the TV on. There was nothing to do, nowhere to be. It almost felt like freedom.

She had started to doze off when there was a knock at the door. She rubbed the sleep from her eyes and stretched. The knocking grew louder. She paused, knowing it could be anyone. Carefully she opened the door leaving it on the latch. Gary leant against the door.

"Mark's not here," she tried to tell him.

He flashed his badge. "This is police business, open the door, please."

Her heart started to sink. He knew she was alone. That was why he was there. She had no choice; he had the authority to kick down the door and haul her into jail. She had to let him in. She took the door off the latch and fell back as he invaded the room, slamming the door shut with malice.

"What do you want?"

He looked her up and down, bile rose in the back of her throat. "I told you, police business."

"So what am I supposed to have done?" She folded her arms, hiding her unease. He just had to mention the word Reacher and she'd be done for.

He was silent. He had nothing on her.

"Get out!" She growled.

He didn't move and he was blocking her only escape, but in the kitchen she had a knife. He anticipated her thinking. As she ran for it he caught her by the hair. She fell to her knees as he withdrew his own blade. The knife scraped the edge of her throat. Her breath hitched. She couldn't swallow. He tightened his grip on her hair.

"You make a noise and I'll cut you," he hissed.

"Is this the only way you can get some, Gary, you have to take it by force because the girls don't think you're pretty enough?" She wasn't going down without a fight.

He punched her. She fell onto the bed, blinking in stars.

"You're not going to get away with this. I'll tell Mark."

"You won't tell him anything. You're never going to see that bastard again."

His hands were experienced. The knife was back at her throat. Without looking he unfastened her trousers, pushing them down to her thighs. How many times had he done this? Too many to be this skilled at it.

"I'm going to hurt you so bad."

Rachel lifted her hand to strike him. He grabbed her, his bare palm squeezing her wrist. "I'm going to hurt you so bad," she snarled back.

He looked confused. His hand started to shake. He made to pull away, but she held him tightly. The knife reverberated against her throat. His body started to quake.

"I'm going to hurt you so bad," she said again.

He couldn't fight it. His mouth choked on his cries. His hand twisted. The knife pointed towards his face.

"I'm going to hurt you so bad!" She screamed.

He cried out, but he could fight it. His arm flung up. He jammed the knife into his neck. Blood spurted like a fountain from the open wound, drenching her. He clenched the handle and tugged it across until the nerves were severed. He fell forward. His body twitched, fighting for life, but he was dying on top of her. She kicked him to the floor and pulled up her trousers.

He was dead in seconds. She'd killed him. She'd killed a cop. There was blood over the bed. There was blood all over her. She reached for Roxy's phone and it slipped out of her hands. She tried to search for John's number and came up with nothing but a list of filthy nicknames she couldn't make any sense of.

Her breath shortened. She'd killed a cop. There was no going back from this. Every police force in the country would be after her now.

28

How long had she been sitting there? The body was still warm. How long did they stay warm? She tried to remember from her study, but her head was in too much of a mess. She didn't hear John and Charlie arrive. Not until John jammed the door closed. Charlie was at her side. He held her head in his hands, he was talking to her, but she couldn't make out what he was saying. She concentrated on the warmth that was growing around her face, grounding herself on the familiarity of him.

"I killed a cop, Charlie," she told him.

"Did he hurt you?"

She frowned; what did that have to do with anything? "Not really. Charlie, he's a cop."

"Don't worry about that. Are you okay?"

She nodded.

"What happened?"

"He's Mark's partner. I think he came here to rape me. He put a knife to my throat so I made him stab himself in the neck. Charlie, he's a cop!"

John rifled through the body. He showed Charlie Gary's police badge and pulled out his phone. Then he stopped. Rachel paused too, listening to the sound out in the corridor. Someone was coming. If it was another cop they were done for. She backed away from the door, but there was nowhere to go. John did the opposite, taking his place alongside the entrance. He nodded at his brother. Charlie stayed by the body, the focal point to anyone entering. The handle started to move. Rachel held her breath as the latch released.

Before he made it into the room John had an arm around the intruder's neck and a gun pressed into his spine. It all happened so quickly Rachel hadn't even seen John move.

"I knew he'd miss me," Roxy said, leaning back into John's stronghold as though this was nothing more than a playful hug. His smile dropped when he saw the mess. "Well, fuck me!"

"Where the hell were you?" Charlie was angry. Angrier than Rachel thought he could ever be.

His tone was enough to unsettle Roxy. Roxy held up the bags of food sheepishly.

"He's one of Pinky's boys," John said tossing the phone back onto the corpse. "Stupid bastard has Pinky Morris in his phonebook."

"What kind of moron does that?" Roxy said.

"What kind of moron goes out for food when they were supposed to be keeping watch?" John snapped back.

"Not now," Charlie said. He brushed the blood soaked hair from Rachel's face. "We're going to need to get you cleaned up, okay?"

Rachel nodded and allowed him to help her up.

"You two deal with this."

Charlie led her into the shower room and closed the door behind them. It was a tight squeeze. He switched the shower on and waited for it to heat up. It didn't. Rachel looked at the water–she'd washed a lot of blood away this week.

"It's going to have to be a cold wash," he murmured to her. "Rach' did he…" Charlie took a deep breath. "Did he touch you?"

"Only once, that was all I needed," she whispered. "Charlie, what am I going to do? There's a dead cop in my flat. They're going to hunt me down."

He smiled and wiped the blood from her face. "Hey, I don't want to freak you out, but that was going to be the case anyway. You're a Reacher and you're throwing your lot in with me and John. We're going to be running for the rest of our lives, but it's okay because I've got your back, and John's got your back. It's going to be okay. We're going to look after you."

She grabbed him and held him tightly.

"Not that I think you actually need our protection, you seem perfectly capable of looking after yourself. Get cleaned up. I'll go find you some clean clothes."

* * *

It was nauseating just thinking about what could have happened to her. Only hours earlier he'd promised to protect her. But she didn't need protecting. Rachel wasn't weak, or vulnerable. She was strong. Stronger than he'd even realised. It was Reachers like her that the government was truly afraid of. And they had good reason to be. It had been a long time since Charlie had come across a Reacher who matched him in strength. This was the first time he'd found one that surpassed him.

He closed the bathroom door. John was on his hands and knees pouring bleach onto the lino. The body was by the door. Some people were great at wrapping presents. John had a particular talent for wrapping bodies. It would be obvious what it was, but people walked bodies out of the tower daily. Why pay funeral costs when there's a perfectly good river you can dump your loved ones into? The main thing was nobody could tell who it was.

"Is she okay?" Roxy asked. Every now and then he would screw up so badly he actually felt guilty. This was one of those times, and Charlie didn't feel inclined to go easy on him.

"No thanks to you," he said. "You were supposed to be looking after her."

"I'd say she did a pretty good job of looking after herself."

"That's not the point. You left her alone. Things might have gone differently. What if she hadn't been able to get close enough to him? Jesus, it's actually a godsend he tried to rape her. There would have been no way she'd have got the upper hand if he hadn't."

"I know. I'm sorry. All I wanted to do was get a good meal inside of her. Poor love hasn't eaten properly in so long. It was stupid, I know, I was showing off and I screwed up."

"Yeah, well, I promised John he could hurt you if you screwed up. I'd say this is pretty high on your list of fuck ups." Charlie rubbed his face. He was getting tired and the smell from the carrier bags of food reminded him he was starving.

"Help John get rid of the corpse."

* * *

Bruises were forming up Rachel's arms. They were the only marks Gary had been able to leave on her. The shower was turning from cold to freezing. Her stomach growled and she remembered the dinner they were supposed to be having. It seemed strange to feel hungry after killing a man.

She was expecting a full house but there was only Charlie, sitting on her stripped bed reading through a file of papers. The body was gone. The blood had been replaced by a suspiciously white stain.

"Where're John and Roxy?" Then she realised. They were getting rid of the body. "I should have helped them. It was my mess."

Charlie put his papers down. "John wouldn't have let you. It's sort of his speciality. Sit down and I'll get you something to eat."

"You don't have to treat me like an invalid. I killed a rapist, maybe I should feel more cut up about it, but I don't," she said.

"It could take a while for the shock to set in."

"Piss off, Charlie. I'm a goddamn doctor and believe me this is nowhere near the worst night of my life. We have real food and a whole night where I don't have to get ready for my shift. Stop worrying, everything is okay."

Charlie smiled. "Fine, then. Go get me some dinner, woman."

With the amount of food in the kitchen there was enough for third and fourth helpings. Rachel heaped their plates high. There was real meat in the rice, real vegetables in the stir fry. It was salty and greasy and heavenly. She nudged Charlie across the bed and sat beside him.

"I can sit on the floor if you want more space," he offered.

She rolled her eyes and gave him a peck on the cheek. "You're a sweetheart, but if you don't stop fussing I will have to make *you* stab yourself in the neck. Besides I like being near you. It reminds me of being back home, with my dad and my sister. Like we're family."

He nodded in agreement. "Did you know you could do that?"

She thought about it. "I've made people drop weapons before at work. I've always thought of it as though I am just planting the idea in their heads. But this was different. He was trying to fight it. I could see him desperately trying to stop his arm from moving, but he couldn't. I was controlling him, Charlie, and there wasn't a damn thing he could do about it."

"Not many people can do what you did." He paused, hesitating on his next sentence. "We're going to break into Pinky's club and rob his safe. Roxy and John were going to go in. Do you want to go with them?"

"I thought you were dead set against putting me in harm's way."

"Yeah, well I think you can handle it. Actually I think they could use you." He handed her his file of papers all written in John's meticulous hand. "John's research and our bible for this job. Mostly it's just what John gathered when we were looking for you, details of the club and Pinky's office, but it's enough to pull off a simple robbery."

Rachel studied the notes on Pinky's office. John had detailed everything, from where Pinky's desk was, to where he was likely to conceal weapons and a safe, to what type of stationery the gangster used. "How'd he get all this?"

"He just sat in Pinky's office," Charlie said with a shrug. "I think he does it to keep his mind occupied. I deal with the client and all the time John is undressing the room with eyes. It's like a hobby, or a compulsion. We didn't even need this information at the time, he just did it because he could. Scary thing is he has all this memorised, he makes the notes for me."

Rachel wondered what the notes on her own flat were like. "Do you have a plan?"

"Working on one, but I need to get Roxy and John past security."

Rachel flipped through the rest of the file. "I can get them in."

29

Roxy was feeling guilty and he didn't like it. He helped John push the cop's body into the river and as it sank the same feeling stirred in his gut. It could easily have been Rachel they were dumping that night. The thought didn't settle with him.

There wasn't an honest soul in his line of work. Thieves, murders, backstabbers; he ticked those boxes himself, without even thinking about his associates, but there was one thing he couldn't tolerate. He'd rather be dumped in a river than work with a rapist. Maybe it was growing up in a brothel, or just having strong women around him all his life, whatever the case, that was Roxy's line and he had nearly crossed it.

He stared at the watery abyss until John flashed the car lights impatiently. Before he could pull away–which he'd done before–Roxy jumped in the passenger seat and waited for the dressing down he was due.

It didn't come. John pulled onto the main road, his gaze concentrating but soft. The silent treatment. Roxy started to squirm. At least when they were arguing it was distracting; they could shout at each other until the veins in John's temples were showing. That was cathartic, that was a release. But it was obviously a luxury John didn't think he deserved.

Roxy couldn't take it anymore. "Aren't you going to tell me how much I screwed up?"

"You're not that much of an idiot, I figure you already know."

Roxy chewed on the dry skin around his thumb, readying himself for an uncharacteristic apology. "I'm sorry. I shouldn't have left her there."

"No. But you did and it was probably the best thing that could have happened."

Roxy frowned, sometimes John's wit got the better of him. "How'd you mean?"

"The way I see it, Rachel had it covered by herself. If you were there floundering around the place, God knows how many bodies I'd be disposing of tonight."

He couldn't tell if John was joking.

"I do not flounder!"

"Of course you don't."

They came to traffic lights. A patrol car was ahead of them. Instinctively John made to go the other way.

"'Least I'm not scared of cops."

"I'm not scared of cops," John snapped.

Roxy pursed his lips. "Prove it."

"What?"

"Rachel's boyfriend stopped by while I was there. And because I do not flounder, I convinced him I was from Counter-terrorism and had a mission for him. He's watching Pinky Morris's warehouse as we speak."

John was silent–brooding over the challenge, Roxy assumed.

"Let's check up on him and see which one of us flounders," Roxy said.

***

Mark had been in the warehouse a good hour before he realised he had absolutely no idea what he was supposed to be doing.

Perched against the small second storey window overlooking the entrance to the neighbouring building, he was pretty sure he was in the right place. He just didn't know who he was supposed to be watching for or why. This wasn't an unfamiliar feeling for him and he assumed he had been told and just forgotten.

He stretched his legs and readjusted his position by the window. He didn't hear the creak behind him, not until it was too late.

"Keep your wits about you, officer," Agent Black said. "You never know who's about."

Mark leapt to his feet. Even in the darkness the red embarrassment on his face glowed brightly. "Sorry sir."

It was then he noticed the second man and for the briefest of moments he thought he was staring death in the face. He started to tremble.

Agent Black handed him a greasy bag. "Hope you're hungry, son."

"Thank you sir," Mark resisted the temptation to open it and start eating. His stomach growled impatiently at him.

"Settle yourself in. You're watching for deliveries going to and from the building next door. Particularly boxes large enough to carry explosives. Mainly we're looking for foreigners. You know what they look like, don't you?"

"Yes sir." Mark hoped he did. There were signs to look for–skin colour, odd clothing. The station had posters up about it in the locker room.

"Don't move from this spot. If they find you don't mention you're a cop. You're not here to make arrests; you're here to get me the license plates of the vehicles and descriptions of the people in the cars. Do you understand?"

"I do sir. You can count on me."

"I know I can, Mark, that's why I picked you. Now give me your phone."

Mark handed over his new mobile and watched as the agent punched his number into it.

"If you run into difficulty, call this number and tell me you are unable to make it home for tea and cake. Say it."

"I am unable to make it home for tea and cake?" Mark tried.

"Good. Use it only if you run into any problems. All being well Agent Smith over here will collect your notes in two days."

"Two days?" Mark straightened up his back. He could make it through two days. It was just sitting in a warehouse and watching. How hard could that be?

"You have a problem with that, officer?"

"No sir. Not at all. Sir, isn't it normal to have two officers on surveillance?"

"Cut backs."

"It's just that my partner, he's a really good guy. He'd be able to give us a hand."

Agent Black shook his head, and Agent Smith seemed to be snarling.

"If you're not up to the job we can find someone else."

"No sir, I can do it, I just…" Mark stopped talking. He was working for the real police now. These men made a difference, and for two days he would too. "I'm up to the job, sir. I won't let you down."

Agent Black patted him on the back. "Well, we'll leave you to it. Remember, eyes peeled. You could be saving countless lives Mark, remember that."

"I will sir."

The agents left. Mark watched for them out of the window but neither appeared. In the distance he heard a car start somewhere. It could have been them, or terrorists. Either way he would watch the window religiously. Every hour of the next two days he would wait in the same spot and witness everything. His eyes started to sting. He blinked his heavy lids closed. No sleeping–that wasn't allowed. Just short naps. No more than two minutes at a time.

They waited outside, watching the warehouse in case Mark got ideas to leave. When they were sure he was staying put John started the car. Roxy knew from years of working with John how much the other man hated cops. In fact, he was pretty sure that disposing of one dead cop and setting up another was probably John's idea of fun. Roxy settled back in the passenger seat, pleased to see that John's earlier hostility was starting to wane.

"See, I was as cool as anything," Roxy teased. "And well done for not buckling under your fear, I know it was tough." He considered putting his hand on John's shoulder, but decided the other man would probably break his hand if he made any sort of physical contact.

John gave him the finger, but there was none of the usual malice behind it. "I can't believe he bought it."

Roxy could. He'd known the minute he'd met Mark that he was just malleable putty in Roxy's hands. "Dumb bastard. You know I am seriously questioning Rachel's taste in men."

John's hands tightened around the steering wheel. Rachel was still a sore topic for him. "I don't imagine she had much say in the matter," he said. "Cop starts paying you attention, what you going to do? Turn him down and let him start wondering why?"

Roxy could see how much Rachel's predicament bothered him. What he wasn't sure of was exactly why.

"You like her, don't you?" Roxy said, fishing for a reaction.

John's eyes narrowed, still unreadable and cryptic. "What makes you say that?"

Roxy shrugged dramatically. "Oh, I don't know. Mostly because you haven't got a bad word to say about her, and I've known you long enough to know that you have a bad word to say about everybody." He expected John to close up, maybe toss an insult his way and spend the rest of the trip in silence. But John surprised him.

"She's got potential," he replied suddenly.

Roxy wasn't sure whether John had missed his insinuations or was just ignoring it. Either way he found himself feeling jealous of Rachel's new found place in the Smith Brothers' cold hearts, especially as he hovered on the sidelines; the black sheep of the Smith enterprise.

"So what–you're banking on her replacing Sarah?" he said bitterly.

John scowled. "No, I don't replace people. Sarah's gone–that's all there is to it. Anyway, if Rachel was going to replace anyone it would be Charlie. Besides, me and Charlie can't find Lilly alone, and she wants to help."

"Meaning I don't." Roxy folded his arms, all of his playful humour gone.

John shrugged, and the insinuation was enough to make Roxy's blood boil.

"Hey, I would do anything for Lillypad. Don't you fucking say that I wouldn't."

John said nothing. Roxy was furious. He had been the only one John could turn to when they needed to get Charlie out of London. Roxy had been there for both brothers against his better judgement until John made it clear that he was no longer needed and no longer welcome. Roxy thought about bringing it all up and throwing it at John to see how the perfect Smith Brother liked being the one in the wrong for a change. But he didn't. He couldn't afford to get into a serious row this late in the game, but he couldn't let John off the hook either.

"Here's an idea. You want Rachel on your team because you fancy a piece of her." It was a childish comment, but he knew it would irritate John.

"I actually have more important things on my mind," John replied coolly. He was trying to act like it didn't bother him, but Roxy knew John, sometimes better than John knew himself–he'd clearly hit a nerve.

"Okay, fine. You're seriously telling me you're not interested in a more intimate relationship with her?"

"Yes." Roxy couldn't tell if he was lying or not.

"Great–then you won't mind if I have a shot then." He grinned victoriously.

"Don't you dare." The threat hung heavy in each word.

Roxy held up his hands defensively. "Hey, if you want first dibs then tell me to back off and I will."

John scoffed. "She has more sense."

"Did you see her ex?" Roxy smirked.

John turned to him, his eyes focussed as though he was trying to calculate the conversation and all its possible outcomes before speaking. "Back off," he finally said.

And if Roxy wanted to keep on John's good side he might have listened.

30

"You have to think of it like a game," Charlie told them. "And winning comes down to knowing the moves, knowing your opponent and luck. There's a board and there are pieces. Rachel is the king, the prize Pinky Morris wants and the one piece we have to protect or it's all over. Rachel will move with you, she'll step up only when she has to. She's by no means useless, but we have to use her in the right way, at the right time.

"Now, John, well he's our queen–shut up Roxy–he's going to be your main cover, the one that's most dangerous, and he'll take out anyone who gets close to either of you."

"Please tell me I'm going to be the bishop," Roxy interrupted excitedly.

"Actually, you're the pawn. You get to the far side of the board without anyone noticing you and you strike down the opposition. While John covers you both, Rachel is going to escort you into Pinky Morris' office and you're going to crack the safe. Assuming you still know how."

"Oh ye of little faith," Roxy replied.

"I'll be waiting in the car. Now, Pinky will be waiting for us to drop Rachel off at the other side of town. If he's a man of his word, he'll be waiting with our money, but I imagine he plans to kill us once we've done the job so the safe should be full.

"You guys get the money and get out. We'll head straight for the border. Cross the city line by the morning. Roxy can bail there and we'll head west."

It was as simple as that. Charlie checked his watch. In twelve hours it would be all over, one way or another.

They packed up Rachel's things, what there was of them, dumping them in the boot of their hired car. Charlie stayed in the flat. He read the file again.

Pinky Morris's life was teetering on the balance of success and failure. If he got Rachel his world would change. He would be powerful again and there would be no stopping him. But, if they did the job right, the tiny blow they were going to strike against him could topple his entire empire. The job was simple, the repercussions were anything but.

"Don't you know that thing backwards by now?" Roxy said.

Charlie looked for the others but Roxy was alone.

"Listen, can I speak to you before we do this?" As he stepped closer he seemed nervous and that made Charlie nervous.

"What's up?"

"I've said some things to you," Roxy clutched at his hair. This was an awkward moment for them both. "Basically I just wanted to say…"

"We're cool," Charlie chipped in before things got weird and uncomfortable.

"Good. Great. It's nice to be back on the team, even without…"

"I know."

"I know I've not been around for you guys, but it doesn't mean I've forgotten about Lilly. I want to help you find her, I owe it to Sarah. My cut from this job, I don't need it Charlie, you take it all."

Charlie was surprised. "You don't have to."

"I do. I'm her godfather, right? And I honestly don't need the money, I'll only spend it on drink and sex and to tell you the truth I can still get a lot of that for free." Roxy paused, steadying himself with a breath. "And I need to do it, to say I'm sorry for how I've been with you."

"Roxy you don't…"

"No, I do. I thought she was just some nutcase you hooked up with, but John told me the truth. She was looking for him; she set you up."

Charlie's mouth became arid. "She came after me because I was weak. It's still my fault. I didn't vet her like I should have done. What am I talking about? I was married–I shouldn't have been sleeping with her in the first place."

"She was from the Institute?"

Charlie nodded.

"I shouldn't have behaved like I did, Charlie. I mean we were friends, good friends, weren't we. Jesus, Sarah used to moan that I got on better with you than I did with her."

"We're still friends, Rox'."

Roxy looked up, his face changed. The mask he usually wore slipped, and he gave Charlie a genuine smile.

"I'm going to do everything I can. You can always count on me to help you get Lilly back."

"I really appreciate that," Charlie was feeling a little choked.

"Just don't tell John, okay. I wouldn't want him changing his bad impression of me. Not when I've been working so hard to piss him off."

Charlie laughed. He couldn't even imagine what John would say if he had heard what Roxy had said.

"I mean it, Charlie. Whatever happens in the future, when you find her you call me, and I'll drop everything to get her out. Whatever it takes."

That was why they worked with Roxy, because despite everything, they could count on him to do what needed to be done.

Rachel and John were downstairs waiting for him. His two-man assault on the rest of the world had become a team again. He dared himself to hope that maybe, if misfortune was turning a blind eye, things might be starting to turn around. But that would depend on the next twelve hours. It would depend on the four of them being able to work together. It would depend on the quality of their opponent. There were too many variables to make this a sure thing. And so much had gone wrong before.

Charlie couldn't believe their luck would change without a fight.

31

Pinky waited in his office, watching the seconds rolling away on the clock. His brother watched him in every photograph. Pinky rapped his fingers on the desk. There was still no news. Something in his gut didn't feel right. He couldn't put his finger on what it was. Charlie wasn't late yet. It could still be all right.

Riva sat on the couch beneath the photographs. She toyed with her mobile, passing it from one hand to the other. The purple bruise on her face was well covered. Pinky stared at it, trying to remember where she had got it.

"You look tense," he said.

She jumped with the sound of his voice. She glanced up at him, wide-eyed. "Tense?"

"Yeah, you look worried."

"I am. Aren't you?"

"What's there to worry about?"

Riva frowned. "What's there to worry about? I don't know, maybe the Smith Brothers double-crossing us. What about Donnie Boom? Jesus, Pinky, what is there to be calm about? And where the hell is Joe? He should have been here by now."

They had a safe full of takings and Joe was supposed to be dealing with it. It wasn't like the guy was always on time; he was heavy and slow and there were a lot of pie shops en route. It was more that Fat Joe was on borrowed time. His heart wasn't good, and one of those pie shops would finish him off any day now. Maybe Fat Joe was in cardiac arrest. The clock kept ticking.

Pinky seemed to be contemplating everything she had said. He stretched and lifted himself away from his desk to sit beside his wife. As he lowered himself onto the sofa he caught Frank's eye again.

Riva tensed up. He reached out and stroked the damaged side of her face. "You worry too much," he said tenderly. "Charlie Smith isn't stupid. If he doesn't deliver I will make sure Donnie blows up that sad excuse for a church, and then I will hunt him and his brother down. He'll give me the girl–you know I've heard about what they've pulled off before, they're professionals–nothing to worry about."

He pushed the strands of loose hair from her face. Riva froze.

"And Donnie, well he isn't going to do anything until he sees the girl and the girl is coming home with us, so he wouldn't be putting any bombs anywhere. And Joe..." Pinky looked once again at the black and white faces of his memory. "Pablo will cover him."

"Pablo?"

"Yeah, call him in. He'll sort the money out."

Riva frowned. She touched her husband's hand with uncertainty. "Pablo's dead."

Pinky thought about it. *Why was Pablo dead?* Then he remembered, of course Pablo was dead. He clapped his hands. "So he is." He started to laugh. "Honestly, what was I thinking? Call Lee in. Good old trusty Lee. We should get a picture of Lee for the wall."

Pinky poked his finger at the faces in the photograph nearest to him. "You know in this picture I'm the only one still alive. Isn't that something? We had it all back then, honey."

"I know."

"No worries back then. You know I hated him, Frank. I hated the fucker."

"I know."

Pinky smiled. He leaned over his wife. "It's going to be all better soon," he whispered, caressing the blemish he had inflicted. His hand shifted to her leg, creeping up her thigh to the edge of her dress.

"Pinky," she warned, but he wasn't listening.

Pinky's phone went off. His hand hovered in the air. He glanced at Riva, excitement flooded his eyes. He looked wild. Fumbling for the phone he snatched it up.

"Yes?"

"We have her," Charlie Smith said. "Where d'you want us?"

Pinky licked his lips. He felt his world beginning to settle. He felt power at his fingertips. "The warehouse," he said. "Bring her there; make sure you're not followed."

"Our money going to be there?" Charlie said.

Pinky's lips pinched into a smirk. "Don't worry, you'll get everything promised to you."

Riva was already at his side. "Do you want me to send my men back to the warehouse?"

He shook his head, "No, keep them at the house. I want to make sure Donnie doesn't get in until I'm ready for him." He sat back in his chair like a rightful king. And he started to laugh.

32

The cop had fucking disappeared. He wasn't answering his phone. He wasn't at home. His goddamn wife wouldn't talk no matter how much Donnie hit her. A sinking feeling in his gut told him that Pinky had already found the girl. That she'd been locked away and he'd never get to ask who did it. That was all he wanted. Seven years of searching and the truth was still an enigma to him.

Someone had killed Frank Morris and Izzy, the two people he loved most in the world. Someone had told him to place that bomb, to set that timer. Someone had sent that text. He was pacing the threadbare carpet of his third storey bedsit. The phone was silent.

For seven long years he had searched for her, picking clues out of the scrap piece of letter. Finding nothing but dead ends everywhere he searched. Approaching Pinky was his last resort and now his second biggest regret. Pinky didn't seem interested in finding his brother's killer. The old man had accepted that Donnie wasn't to blame, but the urgency to find the truth was suddenly secondary to what the girl would bring him.

It didn't make sense to purposefully keep Donnie hidden away like some dirty secret. If there was a traitor, wasn't it better to expose them, to put the pressure on the boys and find out who knew something? Someone would know. Someone sent that text. It went around in his head, over and over, a track caught on repeat, as though the scarring had created a scratch over that one thought in his brain.

Donnie clutched at his hair frantically. The damage to his head had left him with a perpetual headache and tinnitus, and it made thinking difficult.

His phone went off. It was just a message. Not from the cop. This was from Pinky. Donnie's scarred face cracked into a smile. He had her. This was it. He rushed out, forgetting his jacket. The cold wouldn't matter when he got to Riva's. Everything would be righted.

33

"Two minutes to get in the building. Three to get into the office. Four to open the safe. Two to get out."

It didn't give them a lot of time. Rachel tried to control her nerves as Charlie pulled up the car. The edge of London was a short walk away and its wealth was leaking through the cracks of the mesh barrier into the edge of S'aven. The stretch of road was bustling with life from S'aven's affluent and London's trendy youth, slumming it for the night. They were all drawn to the rows of clubs, bars, and takeaways filling every square inch of the street. The Cage pulsated in the centre. It was the darkest, dirtiest of the buildings and drawing the biggest crowd.

The queue into the Cage was swelling into the street the more dusk fell. Inside the party was already raging. Music bellowed out through the small doors, into the street, hitting their car ferociously. Rachel swallowed, her anxiety was growing. She had never seen anything like it and in less than a minute she was going in.

Roxy checked his reflection while John checked his weapons. She just fidgeted, keeping her eyes on the entrance and the two men guarding it. It was her job to get them in, and they were her first obstacle.

"Rach', you sure you're ready for this?"

And she was ready. She wasn't totally confident but she was definitely ready.

"Ready when you are. Two minutes to get in, right?"

Charlie gave them the nod. The countdown started.

John got out the car first. Then Roxy. She sucked in the air around her, embracing the smell of Chinese food and tobacco. If Pinky Morris was waiting for them there was a chance he would see through her mask. But there was also a chance he wouldn't. She looked to John, but he didn't seem worried. She could do this. She had to do this. *Five seconds to get to the door.*

The bouncers were big men, but more fat than muscle. They were on the door for show, more interested in the exposed legs and cleavages on display than any potential intruders. She sized them up and felt tiny, but she wasn't alone. She reached out for John, hooking her arm in his and then did the same with Roxy. *Ten seconds.*

She could do this. She could get them in. *Twelve seconds, two more steps.* The bouncers looked up, confused by the plain girl, wrapped up like she was about to cross the Arctic. Rachel stared at them. *Fourteen seconds.* This was it. *We are important. You're pleased to see us. Open the door, let us in.*

Roxy started to waver, she felt him start to pull away. He didn't think it was going to work. John was steadfast. Drawing on the confidence he had in her she broke free of them both. *Twenty seconds.* She reached out, allowing her fingers to brush over each bouncer. Even beneath their thick jackets she could feel their blood pumping. She smiled and instinctively they smiled back.

"Great to see you," the one on the left suddenly said.

"Come on in," the other added.

"Thanks," Rachel replied as she passed them. *You feel great about this.*

They beamed at her, happier than they had ever been. *Thirty seconds.* They were in. She did it.

Her smile grew with her confidence. She turned to John for praise, but he was already on the move. As she went to follow him she walked into a dancer, and the world materialised around her. The club was wild. Crowds gathered around the band thrashing their weapons against the cage barrier. The music was lost in the distortion but nobody cared. People climbed the tables, the cage, the walls, desperate to get closer to the band or away from the riot erupting on the dance floor. Fights burst from the dancing, and bouncers dived in to deliver concluding blows. Card tables were still dealing hands, roulette tables still spinning. Alcohol flowed like a river and everyone was having a good time whether they liked it or not.

Rachel was pushed into the brawl. She turned, lost amid the faces until a hand pulled her free. John kept tight hold of her.

"You okay?"

"Yeah, this place is crazy."

The Running Game

Roxy laughed. "You think this is crazy you should see it on a Saturday night. Wait here," Roxy shouted. "I'm going to see who we're up against."

Two minutes. Rachel stayed close to John, drawing him into her mask and drawing herself into his protection. He was concentrating on the bar, counting down the minutes in his head. *Two minutes, twenty seconds.*

Roxy weaved his way through the crowd, twisting and turning with what Rachel assumed was the music. The door behind the bar opened and a woman stepped out. Rachel guessed it was Riva Morris leaving. The woman grabbed a set of keys from behind the bar and made her way out the back.

"It's just Riva in," Roxy told them. "Anyone would think luck was on our side tonight. Shall we?"

Rachel took another deep breath, it stank of sweat and blood and beer. *Three minutes.* It was her turn again and she was starting to get cocky. She led them to the bar.

"Wait here," she told John.

The bar was small and overwhelmed by the onslaught of punters. One barman tried to fend off the customers. He didn't even notice when Rachel slipped behind him. She trailed her fingers over the back of his neck and he stopped dead.

"We're going into Pinky's office," she told him. "It's absolutely fine." She smiled, he smiled, and they had their clearance.

She opened the door to the office as though it was her own and stepped aside to let John and Roxy in. Roxy tapped her on the chin impressed.

"Nice work, rookie."

"We're on the clock," John snapped. "Get moving." But he gave her a look, sharing Roxy's sentiments.

Roxy removed a washed out watercolour from the wall, exposing the safe. He flexed his shoulders and got to work. John closed the door, guarding it and keeping his eye on Roxy's fingers.

"Are we on time?" Rachel asked excitedly.

"Ahead of time," Roxy replied.

"Concentrate on the safe. You've only got three and a half minutes left," John snapped.

"You just keep your eyes on the door, Mr Smith, I have everything under control."

It suddenly dawned on Rachel that her sister had been in this room, and this was probably the closest they had been since she came to S'aven. Seven years late, but finally in the right place. She looked for her sister's face in the rows of photographs pinned to the wall. There was no sign of her, just the faces of the men who had abused her. All those men who had had their secrets stolen.

"In ten, nine, eight," Roxy started and winked back at them. "Three, two, one. And who is the greatest safecracker in the world?"

"Fill up the bag and let's go," John said, tapping his foot.

Roxy sang as he worked, stuffing the bag with the wads of cash. There was so much money Rachel couldn't take her eyes off it. Just the sight of it inspired greed in her–if it was this easy they could do it again and again–bags and bags of money...

"Heads up!"

Rachel snapped to attention in time to dodge the bag thrown at John. It bulged with wealth.

"Let's go," John said.

Roxy was still by the safe when Rachel saw the door open. She was too slow and the man standing in the doorway saw her. His eyes met hers and he frowned in confusion until they rolled over to Roxy and the empty safe.

"What the hell are you...?" He was too distracted to notice John at his side. John grabbed his collar and pulled him inside, fixing his hands around the man's mouth and pinning him in place.

"Go!" John ordered them.

Roxy snatched Rachel's hand. He yanked her through the office door. She was about to call out, to tell him they had to go back and help John, but then the music hit her. They had to move. Time was running out. She made them invisible. It was all she could do. Roxy led her away from the exit towards the back of the club. She pulled him back but he insisted.

When she snatched her hand back they were already outside in the alleyway behind the club. Rain had started to fall, dampening the music as soon as the door closed on them.

"What the hell, Roxy? We were supposed to go out the front."

But he wouldn't look at her. There was a gun in his hand; she hadn't even seen him pull it. It hung in his hand, as heavy as the silence between them. He didn't point it at her because he didn't have to.

"Roxy," she reached out to touch him but he backed away.

"Don't Rach'," he murmured.

"What's going on?"

"This way." From the way he said it she knew she didn't have a choice.

Around the corner of the building Riva Morris was standing by her running car. She was waiting for them. Beside her was a tall, scarred man, eyeing Rachel with unnerving enthusiasm.

And Rachel knew exactly what was going on. "You sold us out, didn't you?" She hissed at Roxy.

"Rachel," he said. "I had to, sweetheart."

"You motherfucker! John is going to kill you!"

"Get her in the car," Riva ordered.

The scarred man grabbed her arms, tying her wrists together. He pulled on the restraints until they cut into her skin. She yelled at them. If she yelled loud enough John might hear her. She was bundled into the boot of Riva's car, but the scarred man didn't let her go. His hands pinched into her arms. There was a manic look in his one good eye.

"Frank Morris," he growled, spraying spittle at her. "Who killed him?"

She kicked out at him. "What?"

"Tell me who killed Frank, and this will all be over."

So this was why they wanted her, the whodunit to be solved. All this effort, all this trouble for one stupid murder mystery. She was furious with them.

She leaned forward, drawing him closer. "Fuck you!" She spat at him.

He made to hit her and stopped. The barrel of Roxy's gun was pressed to his neck. The scarred man swallowed, his Adam's apple bobbing nervously against the weapon.

"Don't you dare touch her," Roxy warned.

He glanced at Rachel wedged in the boot and for the briefest moment she thought he was going to save her. But he didn't. He turned away, unable to meet her eye to eye.

"If it's all right with you, Riva, I'll be taking my payment now," Roxy announced.

The scarred man dropped his hand. He turned in confusion, understanding about as much as Rachel did. Then it dawned on her what was going on–the scarred man was the payment. Roxy smacked him across the side of the head, dropping him to the floor. As he bent to pick him up he dared a final look at

Rachel. His eyes were haunted, as though he didn't really want to leave her, but he did anyway, taking the unconscious scarred man with him.

Roxy score two.

34

A satisfying crack came from Lee Hart's neck.

John lowered the body to the floor. He was about to leave, but realised he still had the bag. He frowned. It wasn't like Roxy to forget the money. He grabbed it and slipped out of the office like a shadow. The party outside was undisturbed as he headed quickly towards the front of the building. There was no sign of Rachel or Roxy, but he wasn't sure he would be able to see them even if they were there. So he stuck to the plan and left.

The night air slapped his face and sharpened his senses. He scanned the road, waiting for an ambush. Nothing happened. He heard Charlie start the car and hurried across the road. He pulled open the passenger seat and slipped inside ready to deliver a victorious eyebrow twitch. Only something wasn't right.

Charlie's eyes were wide. He stared at John for an explanation long before he asked the question, "Where's Rachel and Roxy?"

John checked the backseat, just in case his brother had totally lost his head. It was empty.

"They didn't come out?" It didn't make sense. Even if they hit problems on the dance floor they weren't separated for long. John would have seen something.

"No. Nobody has come out since you guys went it. John, what the hell happened?"

"Nothing. We got in no problem. A guy caught us just after we got the money, but I took care of him. They were on their way out about three minutes ago." He paused and suddenly smacked the dashboard. "That son of a…" John opened the bag. He half expected it to be filled with newspaper like the last time Roxy double-crossed them, but the money was still there.

"Money's still there—that's not like him. Hey, what's that?" Charlie plucked an envelope with his name on it from the bag. He showed it to John before he opened it.

Dear Charlie,

Frightfully sorry about this. I'm afraid I have had to take your new recruit and trade her with Pinky for a bit of family vengeance. However, I have full and total confidence that you will be able to retrieve her without much trouble to yourselves. Tell John I'm sorry I had to shoot him, but at least now he knows how much it hurts.

Your ever predictable,

Roxy

"Wait, did he shoot you?"

John gave him a murderous glare. "No, someone saved him the trouble. He's going to wish he had. I'm going back in there."

Charlie grabbed him. "They'll be gone by now, he wouldn't risk hanging around." It was Charlie's turn to hit the dashboard. "Shit. Shit. Shit."

"You know when I tell you next time not to let him in on the fucking job!" John shouted.

"I know, I know. I'm sorry."

"He crossed the line this time," John growled, and Charlie didn't blame him for being pissed off; he was pretty furious himself. All of Roxy's betrayals in the past were about money—he'd find a better deal or just need to pay off more debts than his cut would cover. But this was a cross too far.

Charlie put his hand on his brother's shoulder. "We're going to find her," he said. "Whatever it takes."

John was reverberating with anger, and Charlie knew his brother well enough to know he wasn't going to be able to think straight.

Charlie's hold tightened. "John, listen to me, we are going to get her back because that is what we do. We'll find her and get her out of S'aven. We've already got the money, that's half the job done. Okay?"

John's lips were clenched shut.

"Okay, John?" Charlie tried again.

Finally he nodded, and a look of determination fixed on his face.

"What about Roxy?"

"We'll deal with him."

Charlie started the car, trying to clear his head from the initial panic of losing Rachel. He needed to think straight but nothing about the job made any sense.

Pinky Morris was going to take Rachel and have him and John killed. After all they knew about her; they were liabilities. Charlie could understand that, but Roxy was as much of a threat as they were. He knew who Rachel was and what she could do. Pinky would have to kill him too. So why would Roxy just hand her over? There was only one logical answer: he wasn't working for Pinky.

Charlie thought about the cop and the botched attempt he'd made on Rachel. Pinky was smart; he wouldn't have sent a bumbling wannabe after his prize. The cop must have been hired by someone else. There were too many questions. Too many how's and why's. They shouldn't have taken the case, but Father Darcy had been so enthusiastic. It wasn't like him to even find work for the brothers, but he had, and Charlie didn't want to let him down again. If the old man could only see what a mess he had dragged them into.

Charlie looked up. None of this was right. None of it was ever right. He slammed the car in gear.

"Where are we going?" John asked.

"To church."

35

Rachel saw the gun before she saw anything as the boot was flung open.

It was pointing at her belly; not a good way to go–lots of screaming and agony. She stared down the barrel, seeing only darkness. Riva was in control; the gun was just an extension of her power. The older woman flicked her head, and Rachel realised they weren't alone. Two soldiers reached into the boot. Their dead eyes concentrated on her limbs as they lifted her out of the car.

The night was black, but around them were dull, orange lights, illuminating a large garden, shadowed by soldiers. Rachel tried to count the men guarding the mansion poised in the centre of the grounds. A dozen soldiers, maybe more, walked a beat through the foliage. Their rifles were poised and ready, ignoring her altogether and focusing on the wrought iron gate blockading the entrance. She dared a look back but nobody was there–she smiled inside, hoping Charlie and John were already out of S'aven by now.

"The last thing I want to do is kill you, do you understand?" Riva said, and the soldiers moved away.

Rachel nodded. *The last thing I want you to do is kill me*, she thought to herself.

"We're going to go inside and wait for my husband. You be a good girl, and this will be the best thing that has ever happened to you."

She wanted to be cocky, give the older woman a few snide remarks to show her she wasn't afraid. She didn't. There would be a way out; she just had to wait for it. They had her file, they knew her life, but they didn't know her or what she could do. She intended to keep it that way for as long as she could. *Find the right exit, find the right moment, and then run.*

The Morris house was the grandest thing Rachel had ever seen. She stepped into the lounge as Riva switched on the lights. It was like a room she had seen on TV. Sofas, pictures, a piano. It was elegant and tasteful, or at least it was what Rachel assumed was elegant and tasteful. Riva gestured that she sit down on one of the sofas. It beat the boot for comfort. Rachel sat back, keeping her eye on the gun and Riva's composure. The older woman was still in charge and Rachel didn't doubt that. If she had to, Riva would pull the trigger. She just didn't know what kind of shot Riva was. Would she be able to shoot without killing, maybe just hitting a leg or a shoulder, something painful and non-lethal? She'd fought so hard to get Rachel would she let her go without a fight? From the sofa Rachel tried to understand her kidnapper. Riva was clearly a woman who did what needed to be done. That was how she had managed to have Rachel sitting on her sofa when everyone else had failed. But was she a monster like her husband?

Rachel fiddled with the plastic cutting into her wrists. It was useless, they weren't going to come off. She turned her attention to the room. *Find the right exit.* There were windows big enough to jump through. That and the main door into the room. Even in the dark she could see how long the run to the garden wall was. And if she managed to break out, to leap eight feet over the wall, she had no idea where she was or where she could go.

Riva was watching her. Waiting for her to make a move. Daring her to strike. Rachel placed her hands in her lap. She let her eyes roll around the room nonchalantly. *Let her think you don't care; maybe she'll let her guard down.* Her interest fixed on the photographs in front of her. These were the ones missing from the office. The ones she was looking for.

"Here," Riva lifted a picture of herself and passed it to her. "I think I have more of your sister upstairs. Pinky doesn't like them out."

In the picture Isobel was smiling, leaning against Frank Morris like he was her own flesh and blood. The little girl who had left her at the church all those years ago grew into a beautiful woman with the saddest, pained eyes. All the luxury Frank Morris could give her would never compensate for the life she was forced to live. Rachel ran her finger over her sister's face. She had never known Isobel like this.

"When was the last time you saw her?"

Rachel tried to speak and her voice wavered. She swallowed and tried again. "When I left for the convent."

"You were in a convent?" She was suspicious rather than surprised, as though she had been told something different.

Rachel decided to leave it there. The less they knew about her past the better.

When Riva realised she wasn't going to answer she tried a different question. "Do you know how she died?"

"I was told in an explosion."

"And do you know who killed her?"

"A man called Donnie Boom, apparently."

Riva sat down, keeping the gun poised in Rachel's direction. "The man who put you in the boot, that was Donnie. Only he claims that he was set up. Says that someone told him to plant the bomb there."

"You think I know who it was?"

"Do you?"

"No. Are you going to kill me now? Or are you going to make me whore myself out to all of the suspects until I come up with a hit?"

Riva looked at the picture, a touch of regret gathered in her eyes. "Pinky will ask you. Just tell him exactly what you've just told me. I'll make sure that's the end of the matter. There'll be no whoring you out."

Riva went to the drinks cabinet. She turned her back, watching Rachel through the mirror on the far wall instead. She poured two drinks, subtly checking her watch. Rachel knew the night was by no means over for either of them.

36

The steps above the church were empty, the soldiers were either in bed or in bars. There were no lights on inside the basement church. Darcy would be there, though; he had nowhere else to go. The door was locked. Charlie thought about picking it and changed his mind. There was no point antagonising the old priest if he didn't have to. Instead he banged on the door until he heard movement inside.

There was only an oil lamp lit when Darcy let him in. He expected Darcy to rest it on the altar, so they could speak under Christ as normal, only this time he didn't. They sat at the other side of the shadowy room, and Charlie couldn't shake the feeling that the old priest had been waiting for this moment for a long time.

"We lost Rachel," Charlie confessed before he said anything else.

Darcy didn't seem surprised. "You should have taken her out of S'aven," he said.

Charlie wasn't in the mood for a conversation with hindsight. "We're going to get her back. But there are things I need to know, things I think you've been hiding from me."

"Why would I hide things from you, Charlie?"

"I don't know, because you like screwing with me. Because you think that everything I do in my life is one goddamn parable I need to take a message from."

"Don't blaspheme."

Charlie slammed his hand against the wall and the plaster crumbled in his hand. "I don't know where Rachel is. I don't know for certain why they want her. I don't know who else wants her. And I don't know why they hired us.

But mostly, Darcy, I don't know why you got us this job in the first place. We were supposed to find a girl for a gangster. What is up with that? Since when do you start doing favours for crooks? You're just lucky she turned out to be a Reacher..."

Charlie stopped. He felt his gut sink with the realisation. "You knew she was a Reacher, didn't you?"

He was expecting Darcy to be smug. He expected some spiel about God working in mysterious, vicarious ways. But Darcy wasn't pleased with himself. He cowered back in his creaking wooden chair, avoiding the icon in the darkness.

"How did you know?"

Darcy licked at his cracked lips. He looked like a child, not a man who had stopped an army convoy from storming an Iranian village with one good book and a total disregard for his own safety.

"When Jesus told me to protect you I believed–I still believe–that Reachers are the most important beings God has in this world. Angels on this earth, that is what God told me. I gave everything I could to see your kind safe."

"What did you do?"

"We needed funds, Charlie. The army was clamping down on us and I had people stuck abroad, trying to get Reachers into this country. There were wars, here, there. It was impossible to save you all."

"Damnit, what did you do?"

"I gave Isobel, Rachel's sister, to Frank Morris."

There was only one rule: protect the Reachers. Darcy had instilled that in Charlie and John from the moment he found them. And they had followed it, closer than they followed any deity. For Darcy to have broken it–Darcy who lived by the good book, under Jesus's constant supervision–it was too much.

Charlie leaned forward in disbelief. "You sold her?"

"Frank Morris funded so many operations..."

"You sold her! A Reacher!" Charlie put his head in his hands. "A little girl."

"When I sent the other Reachers out to safety I severed touch with them for their own safety, but I always kept an eye on Isobel. She visited me all the time. She was happy."

"She was being whored out!"

There was no way Darcy had gone through all those years not knowing. Charlie was about to argue. For years he'd listened to Darcy's lectures, watching the old priest ride the moral high ground while he wallowed in a ditch. Now he was looking down on Darcy and the height was giving him vertigo. They didn't have time for blame, or time to recognise that this was the end of their long relationship.

"What is going on, Darcy? Who has Rachel?"

"I don't know who has her now, but she will end up with Pinky Morris one way or another."

"You're sure?"

"Pinky wants to use her like Frank did. The other guy who was after her, Donnie, he's looking for Frank's killer. I'm certain Pinky killed Frank. You go to Pinky and you'll find her. Eventually, they will both meet before this is over."

Charlie stood up, towering over Darcy. Only he didn't feel like he was above the old man, instead he felt like he'd dragged another sorry soul down to his level. He'd introduced Darcy to criminals, he set the righteous man on the wrong path and he left him there to find his own way.

"I convinced them to hire you and John because I knew you would protect her. You are good men, God's chosen ones, both of you. Can you redeem me for what I have done, Charlie?"

The silhouetted Christ was watching Charlie, staring past the bravado, past the disguise.

"I think we're all beyond redemption now, Father."

He left the church.

37

"You know I took Izzy shopping once, in London, just one time in secret," Riva told her. "Frank didn't like letting her out of his sight, but we stole away anyway. It was such a nice day. We got her hair fixed up, some new clothes, had coffee. We could do that, you and I."

"Is that the payment I get for being your whore?" Rachel sipped gingerly at her drink. She had to keep a level head.

"That's not how it's going to work." Riva paused, whirling the brandy around in her glass. "That should have never have happened with Izzy; it was Frank's doing, not ours."

Headlights lit up the curtains. Riva's head lashed around. She took their glasses, returning them to the bar as the front door opened. It was slammed shut. Both women jumped.

"Pinky," Riva called. Her confidence was wavering. She looked to the doorway in uncertainty.

She clearly wasn't a woman who was accustomed to fear. It made Rachel nervous.

Pinky imposed himself on the room. It was the first time Rachel had seen him and for a second she thought he was the man from the photograph. There was the same madness in his eyes, the same fury curling at his lips. He stormed the room, and Rachel was sure he was going to kill them both. He grabbed the gun from Riva's hand and stood in front of her, vibrating with tension.

"I got her for you," Riva said. Her voice was calm and soothing; the rest of her was anything but.

"You went behind my back."

"I put some insurance on the plan, that's all. And look, we have her."

"Who'd you hire?"

Riva hesitated, but caved quickly, "Roxy."

It was the worst answer she could have given him. "Did you kill him?"

"This won't stay a big secret, Pinky. People are going to figure it out. Do you want to be like Frank, going behind the guys' backs? Do you want that to start again?" She gestured to the sofa and placed a daring hand on his chest. "She's here, just like you wanted. Be happy."

He stalked the sofa, inspecting Rachel from a distance. She was too afraid to move. She didn't like this man. Her vision was flashing red, her heart having palpitations. He was bad. He would hurt her. He wanted to hurt her.

"So you're Isobel's little sister." His words felt toxic and hateful.

She didn't say anything. All she wanted was to see Charlie and John again and she felt so guilty for doing so.

"Yes, she is," Riva said for her.

"Your sister was murdered," Pinky told her, almost as though he was taunting her.

"We don't have to do this now. It's late, we're all tired..." Riva began.

"No, we do this now!" He gestured that Rachel get up and she did. "Who killed my brother?"

Rachel stared him in his crazy eyes. "I have no idea," she said coolly.

She didn't feel the slap, but she fell awkwardly on her bound hands. Riva yelled and pushed Pinky aside.

"What the hell are you doing? She doesn't know anything!"

But Pinky didn't know what he was doing. When he hit her Rachel had sensed everything: the paranoia, the fear, the uncertainty. He thought he was losing his mind. Just like his brother. And he was right. The scraps of sanity were slipping away through the hour glass. Time was no longer on his side, and all he could fix upon was his brother's murderer. The brother he hated and loved so intensely he couldn't even separate the feelings.

Riva lifted Rachel back onto the sofa. She touched the slap mark tenderly, trying to repair the damage her husband was causing. She started to speak, but Rachel didn't hear her. She closed her eyes and saw a memory.

Frank's phone sticking out of his coat pocket. He wouldn't miss it, he rarely used the thing. Riva took it. She knew where her brother-in-law would be, she knew exactly when. It was easy. She sent the message to Donnie. There were no regrets.

Rachel blinked and stared at Riva; she killed Frank Morris.

38

The brothers sat outside Pinky Morris' mansion. Charlie thought about what Darcy had said to him. He didn't give a shit who killed Frank Morris. He didn't even care that Darcy had let him down. The only thing that mattered was getting Rachel back. He glanced at his brother, knowing full well that they were both of the same mind. Darcy, Pinky, Roxy; they were just distractions from the only thing that needed to be done: getting Rachel out of S'aven.

They sat in the darkness, parked up against the walled garden, absorbing the glow from the lit up mansion in front of them. The house was twenty yards from the wall, separated by trees, bushes, and the occasional sculpture. Intermittently shadows would pass by–guards patrolling the grounds, the threatening shape of their guns leaving nothing to the imagination.

Somehow they would have to get in through the wrought iron gates or over the eight-foot wall, get across the garden, and take out the guards. If Rachel was there, and Charlie was almost certain she was, they would have to surprise whoever had her.

"No noise," Charlie said, watching as John screwed the silencer on his first pistol.

"Don't worry about it; I'll get her out," John told him, his eyes still fixed on the house.

Charlie pressed his hand against John's shoulder. "Wait, I'm coming with you."

John stopped what he was doing. He looked at his brother uncertainly. "There's a lot of soldiers Charlie. I…" John paused and Charlie knew what his brother meant. He couldn't watch Charlie's back and get Rachel clear.

Charlie smiled. Since he last touched Rachel he was noticing a change in himself. Being close to her reminded him of what he had been–what he was. He could feel the energy now, running through his body with every beat of his heart. He was a Reacher and no back injury or addiction was going to change that.

"I know. That's why you're not going in alone. I've got your back, little brother." He tried to ruffle John's hair and got a slap on the hand with the pistol.

"You'll need this, then," John gave him the pistol and went about setting up another for himself. "Do we have a plan this time?"

"Go in quietly, demobilise any obstacles, pick up Rachel and get back here–if we can do all that without getting shot I'd consider it a win."

John smirked. He put his gun in his holster and flexed his neck. "Then what are we waiting for?"

They got out of the car, pressing the doors closed as softly as they could. Charlie sucked in the air around him, drawing in energy with the breath. He could feel his fingers pulsating, his chest tightening. It felt like coming home, and he revelled in it as they surveyed the wall.

"Not a sound, they can't know we're coming."

"You want to quit talking and get the gate open then, old man," John challenged.

The gate was fixed on an electric lock. All Charlie needed to do was find the charge. He ran his fingers over the metal work, feeling for the electric hum he could manipulate. It was all about energy: feeling it, controlling it, overloading it. It had been so long since Charlie had really used his powers, but it was all coming back to him.

"You going to open that thing or just caress it a little more?" John gibed.

"Screw you. I don't see you vaulting the wall, asshole." Charlie pressed his palm over the pulse of electricity he could feel vibrating through the gate. Nothing was happening.

"Come on, this should be easy." He said it aloud, knowing John was thinking the same.

The gate started to shudder. The rattling ran through to the railings on the wall. Then suddenly the whole thing blew. Sparks fired into the air, chased by plumes of smoke. The gates creaked open, banging against the drive as their hinges twisted and buckled.

Charlie swallowed. So he was a little out of practice, but at least he'd got the thing open. He turned to John, cowering under his younger brother's indignant look.

"Not a sound?" John said with a shake of his head. "I could have just called ahead, let them know we were coming."

They ducked back behind the wall as the guards started moving over to investigate the noise. Charlie leaned against his brother.

"How many?"

"Two on their way down."

"Don't suppose you actually do fancy jumping the wall?"

John sighed. "You're kidding, right?"

"I'll distract them, you take them out."

John jumped the wall like a cat. Charlie didn't even hear him land on the other side but he knew his brother was there, waiting. The guards approached with caution. They kept their voices low, saying only what needed to be said. These were trained professionals—but then so was John.

It would take just one move, but he wasn't sure he could still do it, and if he screwed up—well, it would be his last screw up. Charlie closed his eyes. He thought about Rachel, about Lilly, about Sarah. He stepped into the opening. The guns were raised with his outstretched arm, pointing at his head. He kept his eyes closed, feeling the mechanics of the weapons, freezing them in place. The guards pressed against the triggers—nothing happened. Two slices ripped through the air, shattering their skulls as John fired from the right. They were dead before they hit the ground.

John looked at his brother as though he always knew this moment would come. All the waiting, all the patience had paid off. They were the infamous Smith Brothers and they were not to be reckoned with.

They moved the bodies away from the gate, stashing them in the flowerbeds under the lights. It was time to move. Charlie took the left, his brother the right and in an instant John was lost to the shadows. Charlie didn't need to be so stealthy. He found his next guard alone. With a swipe of his hand the guard's rifle flew into the bushes. Charlie shot him through the head and moved on.

He heard John's shots across the garden, tiny air bubbles bursting in the silent night. Charlie stumbled across another two guards by the fountain. He fired one shot, hitting the guy in the neck, but the other guard ducked the second bullet. Charlie knelt down, hiding in the bushes. He closed his eyes, drawing the energy from the ground. His fist punched the soil and the wave curled across the lawn. The energy pulse hit the guard, pushing him backwards, his body smashed into the fountain. He never came back up to the surface.

Charlie reached the house. He looked to his right to see another guard fall. John was behind him. He gave his brother a nod and they waited. Then the rest of the guards came.

They had trained together but never to work like this. Their partnership was based on experience, on years of dodging the Institute and the cops. Charlie knew exactly what his brother was capable of; there was only one thing he needed to do in return. He raised his arm, counting the weapons and feeling eight of them at his fingertips. He straightened out his arms and waited.

John moved so fast he couldn't be seen. But each movement was calculated and precise. He raised his pistol and shot the men who raised their guns. They fell with a numb thud as their useless weapons betrayed them. The five remaining discarded their guns. John wrapped his hands around the first, twisting his head in one clean jerk. It was effortless for him and more natural than breathing or walking. Six seconds and they were all dead.

Now they had their opening.

39

Riva hugged her, not in affection but to protect her from a beating. Pressed together, Rachel could see everything. Riva killed Frank Morris in cold blood. She calculated the moment he would be at home, she set up Donnie, and she didn't care that Isobel was taken out. Rachel wanted to push her away, and she would have done so too if Pinky wasn't fighting back clenched fists. He was totally lost now. Control had slipped through his fingers one too many times.

"We need to know what happened to Frank!" He muttered more to himself than to them.

"Why, Pinky? Finding out isn't going to bring him back. Don't go ruining what we have like he did. Frank is dead, nothing we do is going to change that. Look, we have her, we have Rachel, we can win again."

"I have to find out."

"Why?"

"Because I need to kill whoever it was. Then people will know I'm not to be messed with. Then they'll know they can't fuck with me anymore!" He pointed the gun at Rachel.

He would shoot her, she was certain of it. It was all about his brother now, not her potential or his future. If she left him hanging he'd see her dead, condemning himself and his empire with it.

"Who killed my brother?"

Rachel had dealt with enough lunatics to know that any answer would shake the final foundation stone in his mental health. His world was crumbling around him and he couldn't get himself free from the landslide. Whoever she said, it would ruin him. She had seen that Riva knew this too and this was what Riva was most afraid of. Not of Pinky finding out the truth and killing her, not the men turning on her. She worried what the knowledge would do to her psychopathic husband's mental health.

He cocked the gun, marking the last three seconds Rachel had.

"I'm going to ask you one more time. Who killed Frank?"

Rachel stared at the barrel. There were times to run and there were times to hide and every so often there was a moment like this. When the exits were sealed and all eyes were on her. She wouldn't die afraid.

She sat forward, untangling herself from Riva. "Your wife killed him," she spat.

He struck her again. This time Riva let him.

"You lying bitch!" He said, grabbing her at the throat. He wasn't going to strangle her though, that wasn't his way. He liked to hit and to punch. He liked to watch people bruise and bleed colour.

"She stole Frank's phone from the club," Rachel said quickly. "Frank was celebrating his and Isobel's anniversary. They had a meal planned. She did it then."

"Shut her up!" Riva yelled. There was too much panic in her voice, and it seemed to fuel Pinky's madness

Rachel clambered away from him.

"She thought Frank was going to kill you. She did it to protect you," Rachel added, but it was too late. Riva's fate was sealed in his eyes.

Riva stepped forward, her arms outstretched ready to embrace him. The gun stopped her.

"Pinky, don't do this."

"You killed my brother?"

"Pinky, put the gun down."

"Did you kill my brother, Riva?"

"Please, darling, please put the gun down and we can talk about this."

"Did you kill Frank?" He screamed.

"Yes! Yes, okay I did it. Someone had to. He was out of control. Ruining everything you had worked for. I saw him looking at you, Pinky, like he did the others. He didn't trust you anymore and I knew it was only a matter of time. I knew you would never hurt him, even if he came at you. I had to protect you, like I've always done. All I ever do is protect you. I love you."

Pinky blinked away the tears. The gun wavered between the women.

Riva braved another step forward. Rachel took one back.

"We can make it good again, darling. Like it used to be. We have Rachel, our very own Reacher. We can be back on top."

He shook his head.

"We can. I promise you."

He raised the gun. He was debating who to kill first. They would both die, but one would have to watch. He made his decision.

The shot shattered the window pane. Rachel flinched. She waited for the pain, but it wasn't her. Riva was screaming. Pinky dropped to the floor. There was a hole in his head and a tiny stream of blood rolling down his nose. His leg twitched and then nothing.

Charlie rested his hand on her arm and she held him tightly. She hadn't even seen them enter. John took Pinky's gun and nudged the body while watching Riva, waiting for her to strike. She didn't. Instead she crawled over to her husband, cradling him in her arms. A minute ago he was ready to kill her. Rachel shook her head; it made no sense.

"Riva," Rachel said and realised she had no idea what to say. She didn't owe her anything, not even pity.

"Get out!" Riva demanded.

Charlie looked to Rachel for guidance before giving John the nod. It didn't matter what she had done, Rachel wasn't about to let an unarmed widow get killed, enough people had died at the hands of the Morris family already.

Cutting her bonds, Charlie took Rachel's hand, feeling another surge of energy and comfort. "Let's get out of here," he told her.

They got to the door before Rachel stopped. She turned back to the dead man and his grieving wife, stepping over the corpse to pick up the picture of her sister. She gave Riva one last cold stare and left the house for good.

"Jesus, look at your face, you nearly look as bad as I do!" Charlie said as he got her in the car. He fussed over her like the old nuns used to do back in the convent. "How bad did they hurt you?"

"It's nothing." She batted his hands away affectionately. "I'm okay, honestly. I can't believe you guys actually came for me, you should have got out of the city when you had the chance."

"You're family now," John stated as though that made their actions any less foolish.

"I'm just sorry we took so long," Charlie said, still trying to check the bruising on her face. "Is that your sister?"

She let him get a better look at the picture. "Yeah, that's Isobel," she ran her finger over the girl in the photograph one last time and put the picture aside. That family was gone now. She glanced up at Charlie and smiled.

John hit the main road out of S'aven, turning the dark streets into a blur of nothing. She noticed him checking her in the mirror after every corner. He looked concerned, and it didn't suit him.

"You okay, John?" She asked.

He ground his teeth. "I'm sorry I let Roxy take you," he said quietly.

"It wasn't your fault. You didn't know Roxy was going to do that."

"I should have," he grumbled.

"Did you get the money?"

He gave her a look through the mirror–of course he got the money. Charlie showed her the bag. It didn't matter that she'd stared down a barrel of a gun for most of the night, that she'd been bundled into the boot of a car and then slapped around by a raving lunatic. None of it mattered because they were alive, they were paid, and they were getting out of S'aven together.

She opened the bag and touched the notes until her fingers brushed something thicker. She pulled out an envelope with her name on it.

"What is it?" Charlie asked.

"I don't know." She opened it and pulled out the identity pass inside. It was exactly like the one she had stolen, only this was filled in and authenticated. There was a picture of her, stamp marks, holograms. It looked genuine. The name read: Rachel Smith and it would get her into London and any other city she dared visit.

There was a note clipped to the back: *sorry, no hard feelings, pet–R -x-*.

"Do you know why he did it?" She asked them.

"Only that he didn't do it for the money," Charlie said with a shrug.

"I think it had something to do with Donnie Boom, but I'm not sure."

"When we see him again you can ask him, right before I kill him," John said.

"It's a shame; we made a good team, the four of us."

She toyed with the pass. With it she had freedom. She was a recognised British citizen with rights to roam the country at her leisure. She couldn't be angry with Roxy, she probably wouldn't be angry with him ever again. The bag of money was one thing, but this, this was exactly what she would have spent her share on.

"I hope it was worth it," she said to herself and she genuinely meant it.

40

Revenge is a festering, destructive mission. Tearing apart the very core of a life for one petty moment when the world is righted, just before the whole thing collapses forever.

Revenge is consuming, eating away at everything else until only it and justice remain. It's too hungry to ever be satisfied, starving with each mouthful. An eye for an eye, a tooth for a tooth.

Revenge can't be cancelled out so easily. There's too much emotional baggage, not enough compromise. But punishment–well, that's different.

Roxy didn't bother with revenge or grudges. He was too lazy for it. But punishment was easy. It was a simple matter of cause and effect. You play with fire–you get burned. You set off a bomb in his mother's club–you get caught in the explosion. An eye for an eye and the matter is dealt with.

"You remember my mother, don't you, Donnie?" Roxy said as he paced the floor of his lockup. "Of course you do, nobody forgets Lulu or her girls. Well, my beloved mum is a huge fan of China. She loves the food, the language, the art. Most of all she loves the fireworks."

Donnie grunted. He was tied to a chair, tape across his mouth. He rocked against the restraints fruitlessly.

"She goes out there at Chinese New Year, watches those babies go up, and BANG!" Roxy pulled out a box and put it just out of Donnie's reach.

"She brought these back after her last trip. Cost a fortune to get them through customs I can tell you, but with Mum when she sees something she's got to have, well she gets it. We were saving them for her birthday. It's next week, but the doctors say she probably won't be out of the hospital for a while yet. I suppose there's no point in wasting them, is there?"

The Running Game

Roxy pulled out a cigarette and his matches. He lit it, watching the flame swell enthusiastically. Realisation set in and Donnie started to panic. Humming to himself, Roxy lit the fuse to the box. He blew out a stream of smoke from the side of his mouth, gave Donnie his winning smile, and he left the lockup. He locked the door and the banging started.

Roxy jumped into his car. He started the engine and cranked up the radio. Dawn was cracking across a purple sky, dissolving under chemical smog. There was nowhere to go, nothing to do. A perfect day to get into trouble. He patted the stuffed tiger wedged into the passenger seat and drove.

Epilogue: Eight Months Later

The first hints of autumn were flashing like a warning sign to the inmates on Work Unit 52. Mark had been working the harvest with the other prisoners, cutting the crops by hand when the machinery broke. There were guards watching him from every direction, watching him and the other twenty men in his team. Sweat was pooling in his eyes as the sun scorched across the grain fields. Soon it wouldn't be hot. Soon it would be so cold he'd look back on these days fondly. Mark had already spent one winter at the work camp, he wasn't sure he could bear another.

The whistle sounded. It was time for lunch. He'd take his measly ration of cold soup and stale bread and eat away from the others. The guards didn't like him, and the prisoners hated him. What was a cop doing in a place like this?

He asked himself the question again and again. They say he'd murdered his partner; stabbed him in the neck and dumped his body in the river. It was ridiculous, but there was blood in his house. Blood and bleach, and Rachel was gone. Mark didn't know what had happened. For eight months he'd churned that night around in his head and still he came up clueless.

A shadow shaded him from the burning sun. Mark looked up, ready to hand over his ration to one of the leaders demanding their fair share. A man in a trench coat stood over him.

"Mark Bellamy?" The voice was commanding, like his old sergeant had been.

"Yes, sir."

"Do you know a woman by the name of Rachel Aaron?"

Mark's heart began to sink. "Is she okay?"

"Come with me, son, we have a lot to discuss."

Dear reader,

We hope you enjoyed reading *The Running Game*. Please take a moment to leave a review in Amazon, even if it's a short one. Your opinion is important to us.

The story continues in *Border Lines*.

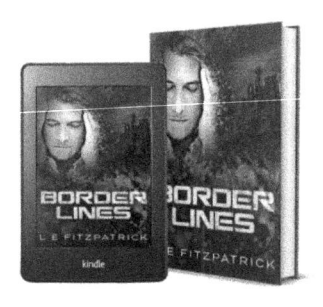

To read first chapter for free, head to:
https://www.nextchapter.pub/books/border-lines-dystopian-thriller

Discover more books by L. E. Fitzpatrick at
https://www.nextchapter.pub/authors/le-fitzpatrick-science-fiction-author

Want to know when one of our books is free or discounted for Kindle? Join the newsletter at http://eepurl.com/bqqB3H

Best regards,

L. E. Fitzpatrick and the Next Chapter Team

Acknowledgements

Many people were involved in the making of this story over the past four years. To start with I'd like to thank all my incredible beta readers who picked up my first draft and offered such kind words of encouragement all those years ago. I'd like to thank Alina for all her hard work promoting me back when I was a struggling indie and making me believe in my work. Thanks to the readers and supporters of the Reacher series, who kept me going when I wanted to give up. A huge thanks to; Jennifer, Carol, Ashley, Majanka and Belle for all the hard work you have put in and for bearing with me. Seriously guys, you're all amazing. Also huge thanks to Miika and Creativia for taking a shot on me at a difficult time. As well as hugs to the #Awethors and the online community who continue to have my back through the good and bad.

Finally a big "diolch yn fawr" to my long suffering family, who have supported, tolerated and encouraged me throughout this whole journey. Sorry – this is a series so we've still got a few more torturous years to go.

About the Author

L E Fitzpatrick is a writer of dark adventure stories and thrillers. Under the watchful eye of her beloved rescue Staffordshire Bull Terrier, she leaps from trains and climbs down buildings, all from the front room of a tiny cottage in the middle of the Welsh countryside.

Inspired by cult film and TV, L E Fitzpatrick's fiction is a collection of twisted worlds and realities, broken characters, and high action. She enjoys pushing the boundaries of her imagination and creating hugely entertaining stories.

www.lefitzpatrick.com

Lightning Source UK Ltd.
Milton Keynes UK
UKHW011031090820
367887UK00005B/135